MYTHIC

A QUARTERLY SCIENCE FICTION & FANTASY MAGAZINE

ISSUE #2 | SPRING 2017

TABLE OF CONTENTS

GW00493179

MYTHIC
A Quarterly Science Fiction & Fantasy Magazine
ISSUE # 2 SPRING 2017

Published by Founders House Publishing LLC

MYTHIC: A Quarterly Science Fiction & Fantasy Magazine
is a project and publication of Founders House Publishing LLC.

www.mythicmag.com

www.foundershousepublishing.com

ISBN 13: 978-1-945810-05-3
ISBN 10: 1-945810-05-X

Printed in the United States of America

MYTHIC is quarterly magazine published by Founders House Publishing LLC. We publish speculative fiction, specifically science fiction and fantasy. Our mission is to expand the range of what is currently possible within both genres. We like new perspectives and new spins on familiar tropes. Diversity is a hallmark of our vision.

One year, four-issue subscriptions to *MYTHIC* cost *$40*. You can subscribe by visiting www.mythicmag.com or make out checks to Founders House Publishing and send them to the following address: 614 Wayne Street, Suite 200A / Danville, IL 61832

If you are interested in submitting to *MYTHIC*, you can visit our website for information regarding our submission guidelines.

www.mythicmag.com/submissions.html

MYTHIC: A QUARTERLY SCIENCE FICTION & FANTASY MAGAZINE

EDITED AND DESIGNED BY
SHAUN KILGORE

———

SPECIAL THANKS TO OUR SUBSCRIBERS AND PATRONS ON PATREON:

YOU HELP MAKE MYTHIC
BETTER ONE ISSUE AT A TIME.

(www.patreon.com/mythicmag)

Coming Next Issue in *MYTHIC*

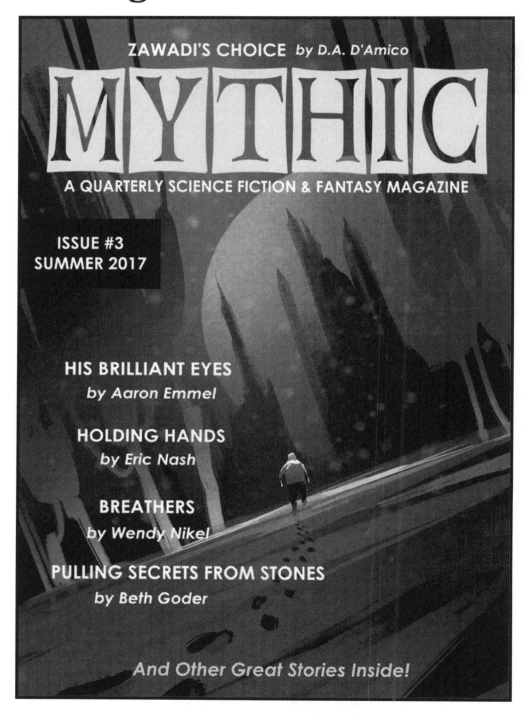

ZAWADI'S CHOICE *by D.A. D'Amico*

MYTHIC

A QUARTERLY SCIENCE FICTION & FANTASY MAGAZINE

ISSUE #3
SUMMER 2017

And Other Great Stories Inside!

INTRODUCTION
LESSONS LEARNED

BY SHAUN KILGORE

Greetings sci-fi and fantasy fans. I want to you welcome to the second issue of *MYTHIC: A Quarterly Science Fiction & Fantasy Magazine.*

With any worthwhile endeavor, there is, more often than not, some kind of learning curve—and with creative projects like MYTHIC, that is definitely true. There are plenty of details that need to be worked out with a magazine like this one. Not only do I, as editor, have to do my best to choose a great selection of stories, a broad sampling of the genres that gives just enough variety to the content appearing every quarter. There are logistical and scheduling processes that go into the formatting and presentation of the content and in the appearance of the publication.

I'm happy to say I'm making progress and I've learned a few lessons. There is still much more to this curve I'm on but I'm forging ahead and doing my best to make MYTHIC a better magazine, issue by issue.

I'd like to give my thanks to the early supporters to this project. The subscribers, the folks who've chosen to back us via Patreon, and especially, the authors. I've had the sometimes difficult task of choosing from among the efforts of some very able and creative scribes in order to find the small selection of stories to appear in these pages. Without all of you, MYTHIC wouldn't exist.

Dear readers, I hope that you enjoy reading the stories as much as I did. If you like what we're doing, please support us. Spread the word about MYTHIC. Help us make this magazine better. We would love to improve our rates for authors, the life's blood of any publication like this. Thank you again.

Interested in submitting stories to MYTHIC? E-submissions may be sent to **submissions@mythicmag.com**. For complete guidelines, visit us at: **www.mythicmag.com**

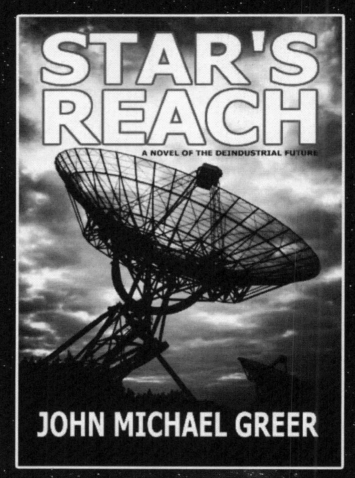

THE KINDLY ONES

BY ELANA GOMEL

The world ended on the day my husband brought me flowers.

It started as usual: Karen and Andrew fighting in the kitchen, the TV volume going up and down like the sonogram of a heart attack. As I rushed down, there was a crash. I found them contemplating the shards of a bowl and the TV remote gently sinking into a puddle of milky cereals on the floor. I rescued it and they both backed away, their temporary truce re-established when they saw my face.

I had no energy for yelling at them. I had slept badly. The dream had returned and I spent two hours watching the furry branches of our Douglas fir claw the red-tinged darkness. Martin was snoring gently and I longed to snuggle up to him but was afraid of interrupting whatever mysterious calculations went on in his sleeping brain.

He was in the living room, drinking coffee and staring intently at his computer. When I put my arms around him, he twitched as if bothered by a fly. Nor did he react when the kids called out in unison, "Bye, Daddy!" as I shepherded them toward the car. An ordinary morning, in other words.

When I came back he was gone and I had the house to myself. These couple of hours in the morning, contemplating the pristine expanse of seemingly unlimited time ahead of me, is what keeps me sane. There are so many things I can do, so many projects I can accomplish, while the twins are at their Montessori pre-school and Martin at work. The feeling is normally gone by the time I have mopped up the puddles on the kitchen counter and have taken a stab at the chaos in the twins' rooms.

It was the same that day except there was something else nagging at me. The dream.

The mindless drone of the TV was getting on my nerves and I was about to turn it off when I glanced at the Breaking News at the bottom of the screen. It said: 'The massacre in Shanghai."

That was it: just this one phrase. I blinked and it was gone. The talking heads went on.

I was born in Shanghai and I had never seen it. My parents had worked for Rockwell. They left China when I was two months old.

I went to the computer, clicked on Google images of Shanghai and was rewarded by a kaleidoscope of lights and crowds, the Bund awash in dancing neon. Somehow I was reassured. I promised myself one day, when the kids were older, we would all go there.

The relevant headline was not at the very top. It simply said that about twenty people had been killed in what appeared to be street riots in Shanghai and several other Chinese cities. *SF Chronicle*, catering to the city's large Chinese population, was more expansive but not more informative.

Then it was the time to fetch Karen and Andrew. They started bickering in the car and I ground my teeth to keep myself from spewing out all the venom that had accumulated since their birth in my flabby post-Caesarian belly.

They calmed down later in the afternoon and I let them watch cartoons as I cooked dinner. I had to scrap my first attempt at ragout because I forgot Martin's instructions and added too much salt. Since going vegetarian,

he had become very particular about such things.

As I chopped onions for the second round, I let my mind wander. I always wanted to live in the city. But SF is so prohibitively expensive, and the twins' schools...

There was silence in the living room and it woke me from my reverie. Andrew toddled in, clutching a red-stained kitchen knife.

"I cut tomatoes for you, Mummy!" he said proudly.

I hugged him and pried the knife away. Karen was sprawling on the floor, busily mutilating an eggplant. Martin would never eat anything else than perfectly cut, perfectly cooked vegetables but I was suddenly glowing with rebellious pride. They were my kids and they loved me. I let them help.

The dinner—version number three—was still cooking when he came through the door, clutching an enormous bouquet of yellow roses. The kids and I watched him open-mouthed.

He hugged me, kissed the twins, and asked about our day. They were so flabbergasted that they finished their mini-burgers in silence. It took a protracted battle to convince Martin that their growing bodies needed animal protein.

I married Martin because I wanted to understand him. Finding out that it was impossible did not make me regret my decision. Martin was a mathematical genius and borderline Asperger's. He knew that he was smarter than most people and let them know it too.

But now he was nodding and smiling. It was unnerving. Also unnerving—because unusual—was the fact that he had turned down the lights in our bedroom so low that I could barely see his face. Normally he spent exactly twenty minutes in bed reviewing the latest issue of *Algebra and Number Theory* before becoming aware of my presence.

"Hon," I asked, "have you heard about the riots in China?"

"Yes," he said in his beautiful voice that even now, after six years of marriage, managed to send shivers down my spine.

"What do you think?"

"The cities are emptying."

"Why?"

"Too many people. Strangers, looking at each other. It creates tension."

While I was trying to figure out what the hell it meant, he reached for me and I forgot all about urban living.

The dream came again but this time I woke right in the middle of it and so it remained as fresh as a bleeding wound.

The dream had appeared when I was fifteen, going through my first heartbreak (one of many) and came back from time to time, just to keep me company, I suppose. But now it had reinvented itself, apparently absorbing the strange conversation I had had with Martin.

In the dream I walk through my parents' house in Sausalito. Clammy fog is swirling outside and when I run my fingers on the counter, they come off wet. Everything is dripping, waterlogged, rotten-soft as if the house just emerged from the Bay.

My feet carry me to the den. The TV is on and my mother's blond curls show above the back of her favorite antique armchair.

I pray she won't notice my presence but she does. The armchair slowly swivels around and she smiles at me, as she seldom did.

She cannot *not* smile. The rotting flesh of her face hangs in tatters over the grin of her exposed teeth. The empty eye sockets stare past me.

"Mommy!" I cry.

And then she looks at me. The stringy neck tenses and the skull turns as those black holes target me. There are no eyes in them. But she sees me.

She is getting up, creakily, and pieces of her fall onto the floor.

My mother died when I was twenty-one, of lung cancer, but the dream took no notice of this fact, repeating the zombie show with the same dogged persistence until I was numbed to it. And it was not that I had been particularly close to her.

Still, I missed her. Occasionally.

But there was a new addition to the dream that nagged at me as I lay in darkness, listening to my galloping heart.

Over her skeletal shoulder I had seen images on the TV. It showed a city street full of people: a dense crowd flowing between the concrete banks of skyscrapers. People walked along, bumped into each other, squeezed through dense vortices of bodies. It looked like Shanghai or maybe Market Street in San Francisco on a parade day. But everybody on the street had a blindfold made of whatever was at hand: rags, towels, pieces of clothing.

My father called next morning. He had taken early retirement after my mother's death and was now living in the old house in Sausalito with a new girlfriend. It is amazing how people repeat the same mistake over and over again. I had often wondered what made him marry my mother whose idea of a family dinner was a takeout in front of the muted TV, while she leafed through an untidy pile of work files. She had been CFO for a high-tech company and had precious little life outside that role. To be fair, she had made a pile of money some of which went into my trust fund. Despite it, my father had not been happy, suffering our fragmented family life in gloomy silence. You'd expect him to find a cheerful homebody. Instead, Lydia, his current girlfriend, was a younger, thinner, hungrier version of my mother, focused with laser precision on her career as a software engineer. She was not bad-looking but had all the social graces of a badger.

Dad sounded uncharacteristically anxious. After some hemming and hawing he came down to business.

"Ida," he said, "there is something wrong with Lydia."

I of course instantly assumed she had left him. I was trying to think how to phrase it diplomatically when he delivered his surprise line:

"She is too kind."

I thought I had misheard.

"Wild?"

"No, kind. I'm telling you, it's spooky. She started cooking dinners."

"So? What's wrong with that? You don't like her cooking?"

"No, it's not that. It's...unnatural somehow. It's not her. I mean...Ida, would you come over? And bring the twins. I miss them."

I should have known better. But at the end I agreed. I packed the kids into the Volvo and we drove across Bay Bridge.

The morning was cold and raw, one of those San Francisco mornings when the city hankers down like a bag lady, pulls its ragged veils of swirling fog over its head and refuses to look at you. Its beauty suddenly turns into surly ugliness, its vitality—into hushed paranoia.

The streets were empty but the sidewalks were littered with piles of garbage, indistinct shapes stirring among the litter like moths hatching from giant cocoons.

When I pulled into my father's driveway, Lydia stepped outside. It was surprising: I had never known her miss a day of work. Even more surprising was the broad smile on her face when she saw the twins. She hugged them and cooed.

I began to understand Dad's misgivings.

She plied the kids with the goodies forbidden in our household: soda and candy. I did not object because I was afraid.

I did not know what I was afraid of: the cold gray sky, Lydia's unwavering smile, or her assurance that Dad had just gone out for a drive to the Marin headlands and would be back in half an hour at most. Every single piece of this morning was perfectly ordinary; together, they made a pic-

ture that was as distorted as a reflection in choppy water.

She made coffee. She gave me homemade *pan dulce*. I could not swallow it and yet I knew I must. I kept my eyes away from her cheerful face, unwilling to see something I did not want to see. It probably saved my life.

I excused myself and went to the bathroom. On my way, I passed the den and saw my mother's old armchair, the one in the dream. Dad had kept it.

My eyes filled with sudden tears. Mom was cold, distant, self-absorbed. But she had loved me. I knew she had.

Suddenly I realized what was so different about this new Lydia.

I pulled out my phone and speed-dialed my father's number. It rang and went to his answering service. Only when I pressed 'Stop' did it occur to me that the ring-tone was double. I could hear it in my ear but I also heard a faint echo of it coming from somewhere above.

I ran up the stairs to the master bedroom, pushing the button again. The ring-tone was coming from the en suite bathroom. I slammed the door open.

My father was wedged into the narrow space between the tub and the toilet, the towels wrapped around his head stiff with maroon splotches. His body looked as ungainly as a puppet's, one arm hanging over the lip of the tub like a discarded brush.

Shock makes you clear-headed and detached. I did not touch him. I heard the twins' voices and then Lydia's laughter. It sounded completely natural.

I closed the door and crept downstairs. They were in the living-room, sprawling together on the floor. She was showing them some new game on her iPad.

"We are going home," I declared, overriding their protests. "Daddy is back and waiting for us."

It was a lie but it worked.

Lydia got up, brushed her black jeans.

"Ida," she said, "are you OK? You look a little shaken. Do you want me to drive you back?"

I mumbled something negative, gathered the kids, practically dragging them to the door. My hands shook.

But I felt no tingling at the back of my head as I bundled the twins into the car and careened out of the driveway, with Lydia standing at the door, watching us. They say you can feel when somebody is staring at you and this is true: I know it from experience.

But I could not feel Lydia's gaze. She was looking at me but she was not seeing me. This was what I had noticed when I came in but it took time to sink in because it was so strange.

Her eyes were not glazed; she was not inattentive or distracted. Just the opposite, she seemed to be entirely focused on me, hanging on to my every word. She responded appropriately to whatever I said.

And yet I knew that she neither saw nor heard me.

I was not trying to resolve this paradox as we drove wildly back home. I was trying to keep a lid on my panic. It was still chilly and gloomy: as opposed to the usual Bay pattern, the fog did not lift. I felt as if I were in a foreign country. And I was.

Somehow I ended up on the Golden Gate Bridge, even though I normally try to avoid its congestion. But there was none today. There were few cars, no pedestrians, despite the fact that people always walk and jog on the most beautiful bridge in the country. But there was something hanging from one of the orange-red beams. A bundle of rags. A large bundle of rags.

I prayed the kids would not notice it and they did not seem to. They sat in their car seats as quiet and well-behaved as a pair of dolls. I glanced at them and felt whatever was left of my sanity crumble.

I pulled off at the deserted transit plaza and called Martin. I knew I should have called 911 but I had a hunch that they would not answer. Neither did he.

I would have gone to the city center—Market, SoMa—just to see what was going on. I was beginning to understand how all the horror films I used to despise were true. The heroine does walk down into the dark basement alone even though she knows the monster is there. There is that irresistible human compulsion to see. To see is to understand. Understanding is power. Even if you are killed by the monster, you master it when you see it.

But I had my kids with me. And so I drove back the same way we had come in, through the quiet residential streets. Only they were quieter than usual because all the homeless people I had seen on the way in were stacked two or three deep on the pavement, now cleaned of the litter. Fortunately, they could pass for some neighborhood Goodwill drive because their faces were carefully swathed in torn scarves, towels, rags or whatever else the killers could lay their hands on. They looked like bundles of discarded clothes. They did not look human. But if the kids asked what they were, could I deny these pitiful remains the dignity of acknowledging their humanity?

They did not ask.

At home I turned on the TV, the computers, the radio. There was white noise everywhere. The servers were down. I called all the numbers in my address book and got no connection.

I fed the kids, trying to pretend everything was normal, and with every second my horror grew because they were buying it. They behaved better than they had ever done since the moment of their raucous birth. They did not squabble. They ate their vegetables. They sat down to the long-abandoned board game.

I could not stand it anymore.

'Karen! Andrew!'

They looked at me: two pairs of round, innocent brown eyes. Attentive and kind. And blind.

I don't remember what happened next but I found myself in the kitchen, cradling a half-empty whiskey bottle. I was not drunk, though. I heard when the garage door opened.

I was clutching the largest kitchen knife when Martin walked in. For the first time in my anti-NRA life I was sorry we did not have a gun at home. I looked at the stranger who had stolen my husband's beautiful distracted face and realized I would have no compunction in shooting him.

"Honey!" He walked toward me, deep concern in every feature— except the eyes. You cannot feel concern for somebody you do not see.

"Dad!" the twins spilled into the kitchen and he lifted Andrew into the air, spun him around, the little boy laughing. I let the knife drop.

They look like my family. They talk like my family. Who am I to say they are not them?

I am standing in the kitchen, counting seconds until the timer rings. The seductive smell of freshly-baked buns wafts through the air. The steaks are ready. Laughter and snatches of talk come from the living room where Martin is entertaining our guests: a couple next door, Jim and Kelly, and Lydia with her new partner. The kids are playing with Kelly's five-year-old daughter. In the past I would have been on the edge foreseeing an accident or a fight, listening for the sounds of distress from the kids' rooms. Not now.

Martin shows up, a broad smile on his face, holding a glass of Pinot Grigio.

"Mm! Smells good!"

He puts his arms around me and I feel my body respond, predictably and humiliatingly. The body is dumb; it does not know what I know.

"It's almost ready," I say and squeeze icing on the buns, delaying the moment I have to walk back to my guests. Martin pours me a glass of wine and stands there, watching me do my household chores. When he is not smiling, he almost looks like my husband.

"Why didn't you kill me?" I ask, suddenly sick of the entire charade. Perhaps the wine has gone to my head.

I expect him to look through me blankly as they all do but his reaction is different, suddenly bringing back echoes of the prickly unpredictable man I had married. He frowns thoughtfully.

"I don't know," he says.

It is the first time he—or anybody else—has admitted that fifty per cent of the population are gone. My hand twitches, the pink icing dripping on the floor. Martin tears off a paper towel and gets down on his knees to clean up the spill.

"Are you aliens?" I ask.

Lydia dances into the kitchen, her eyes bright, her breasts filling her tight top. She had put on weight.

"Ida, honey!" She cries. "What a miracle cook you are! Look at these yummy buns!"

Finally, when they are all gone and the twins are tucked in, I steal into the den and turn on the computer. After those twenty-four hours of total blackout, communications were restored. Sort of. The Internet is a pale shadow of its former infinite self, the number of sites down drastically, servers malfunctioning, familiar sites filled with nonsense or flashing signs in strange languages.

But images search still works. I click on the latest item in history. And I am staring again at pictures of the empty city, the Pearl Tower dark against the lowering sky, the muddy waters of the Yangtze River lapping at the dark Bund.

All the major cities are like this. Abandoned. Deserted. The greatest genocide in human history and nobody gives a damn. Maybe because there is nobody left to give a damn.

I remember an article I had read. Long time ago, before it all started. The author postulated something he called a philosophical zombie. Imagine a creature who acts and responds like a human being but has no self-awareness, no self at all.

A zombie invasion did happen, like all *The Walking Dead* clones predicted. But these zombies did not chomp on human flesh; they just ate our minds. Perhaps I am the last self-aware human being left.

But as I sit in the darkened house, staring at the screen, doubts begin to assail me. How would I know? How is it possible to know that another human being is *not* a mindless automaton, going through the motions? Maybe it has always been like this and I have just woken up to reality.

No, it can't be. The cities have been emptied. Millions—billions perhaps—have died. Their pretense that the things are as usual is the best proof that they are not.

Why did they kill the urban dwellers? Perhaps because in the city you cannot avoid looking at strangers and being looked at. And they do not like being looked at. They know we can see the emptiness in their eyes. Mind-blindness. Because they have no minds.

And they are kind, much kinder than the people they have displaced. My husband is attentive and affectionate. My kids are picture-perfect.

I am trying to figure out why. Perhaps because they are just obeying the behavioral routines programmed into their brains. No angry self to lash out against annoying and restricting others. And no forgiving self to surprise with a sudden contrition.

But they are dangerous. I keep seeing my father, his face wrapped in bloody rags as were the faces of all the victims. They cannot bear to be looked at, even by the dead.

I feel the presence at my back and turn around slowly, expecting to encounter the new Martin's toothy smile.

But it is not Martin. It is Andrew.

"Mum," he says, "it's late. You'll feel bad tomorrow."

This caring adult voice, this soft hand on my shoulder—this is not my son. I let him take my hand and lead me to the bedroom. As we are walking up the stairs, I am suddenly convinced I'll never see the light of dawn. The zombies will kill me.

Or maybe not. Maybe they'll let me live just to witness their brave new world: without cruelty, conflict, war. Without passion or longing. Without cities.

Or maybe they don't even know the difference between me and them.

"Good night, mommy!" Andrew says and waits by the door as I step into the impenetrable blackness of the bedroom.

I pray that I dream the dream again. My mother will look at me with her dead eyes and will see me for what I am.

About the Author

Elana Gomel is the author of five non-fiction books and numerous articles on subjects ranging from science fiction and fantasy to posthumanism and Victorian literature. Her stories appeared in *New Horizons, Aoife's Kiss, Bewildering Stories, Timeless Tales, The Singularity, Dark Fire* and other journals; and in several anthologies, including the *Apex Book of World Science Fiction*. Her fantasy novel *A Tale of Three Cities* was published by Dark Quest Books in 2013. She can be found on Facebook and on Twitter as @ElanaGomel.

Don't Miss an Issue!

LOYALIST PROTOCOL

BY PATRICK S. BAKER

The captain growled and shot a look at the junior engineering officer in the CAC, Lieutenant Renko merely smiled, drew a hidden sidearm and shot the captain in the face with the old fashioned slug-thrower.

Commander Lumaban Ilocano, Executive Officer of the Solar Union Defense Force Sword-class heavy cruiser *Grus,* had been sitting quietly at the damage-control station in the Command Action Center as the captain ran another battle-drill. The crew and the captain were new to the ship, so Captain Hallie was taking the opportunity to shakedown the ship and crew while the cruiser plowed through normal space in the outer reaches of the Delta Pavonis system.

"All stations report ready, except engineering," the operations officer, Lieutenant-Commander Ito said.

Captain Hallie started to say something to Renko, when the junior officer killed the captain. Renko then turned and shot Ito in forehead, flinging the ops officer against his console. Lumaban jumped up while the rest of the CAC officers were frozen in place by the sudden violence. The murderous officer shot the XO. The impact pitched the senior man back and knocked his head against the Damage Control station. He slid down and landed with a thump on the deck.

The XO came to and saw Renko sitting in the command chair, with Captain Hallie's body on the deck at Renko's feet.

"Ship, release the door and let Lieutenant-Commander Bowen in to the CAC," Renko said. "He is the senior officer and therefore the acting commanding officer."

"No," the Human Artificial Intelligence Linkage System responded, in a softly feminine voice. "You and Bowen are mutineers."

Lumaban sat up slowly, unseen by the mutinous lieutenant. His head and shoulder hurt like he'd been beaten with a cricket bat, but the bullet had struck his combat suit just below his exposed neck and had not penetrated. Lumaban didn't wait, he crept slowly

17

toward Renko, whose back was turned. The murderer continued to argue with the ship.

Lumaban jumped up, locked his right forearm around Renko's neck and dropped down, using his weight to pull the seditious lieutenant down against the fulcrum of the chair's back. Renko's neck snapped. The commander stood, breathing heavily. His grandfather had been a Solar Union Marine and had taught him Kali fighting techniques, but this was the first time he'd every used them outside of practice, or a fighting ring. This was the first time he'd killed a human. He heaved the lieutenant's dead body out of the command chair and sat down.

Looking around, Lumaban and saw that Renko had shot the rest of the CAC crew. Suddenly, he felt less bad about breaking the *anak sa ligaw* neck.

"*Grus*, what is happening?" the XO asked the ship as he picked up Renko's weapon.

"A mutiny," the ship responded. "The first mutiny ever of a Solar Union warship. On a preset signal, several members of the crew killed their crewmates and seized control of almost all of me. The only loyal holdouts are in weapons' control and the boat bays. Chief Engineer Lieutenant-Commander Earl Bowen appears to be the leader."

"Get me coms to Bowen."

"Aye, sir. He's right outside the hatch."

"Earl, it's me, Lumaban. Why are you doing this?"

"Well, XO, you're alive," Bowen said, surprised. "I told Renko to shoot you right after he shot the captain. Guess the best laid plans and all that," the mutineer leader said, like he was giving a formal briefing. "It's the treaty, of course. We're just giving two whole planetary systems to the Corvo after how many good humans bled and died for them? Over forty thousand dead in this war."

"Earl, the treaty ends ten years of war and we get two other and better systems," Lumaban said. "It is as fair as those things can be. Besides we're Solar Union Defense Forces. No politics in the Forces, remember. We're subordinate to the elected civilian leadership. Do you want to go back to the times when military juntas were running whole regions like before the Unification Wars?"

"I don't care. My brother and sister died at Second Kisshoten, We can't let their deaths for nothing."

The SUDF was a family business with children often following parents or siblings into the Forces. Loses felt like deaths in the family.

"Every one of us lost someone in the war. My nephew died on Budia. This is not the way to honor them.

Besides what can one heavy cruiser do?"

"You think this is only ship with real loyalists on it. When this is done we'll have a whole fleet. Then we'll take back Kisshoten and Faraway."

"Sir," *Grus* said to Lumaban. "I have blocked them from bypassing the door locks. But they're bringing in a cutting torch. They'll be in the CAC in about twenty minutes. The mutineers have also seized weapons control and executed the loyal crew members. The weapons crew sabotaged the firing stations."

"Earl, you *anak sa ligaw*, stop your mutineers from killing their crew-mates!"

"Sorry, but sacrifices have to be made," Bowen said with no inflection. "I don't suppose you'd consider joining us?"

"*Mamatay ka sana!*"

"What's that mean?"

"Go to hell!" the XO said and cut the connection without waiting for Bowen's response.

"*Grus*," Lumaban said. "Put me through to the loyal crew in the boat bays."

"Aye, sir. Chief Cobb is in charge there."

"Chief," the XO said. "This is in Commander Ilocano."

"Yes, sir."

"You are ordered to abandon ship and sabotage any boats you can't take with you. Head for Sanxing, you should be able to make it. But you are to go, now."

"But sir. . ." the chief started.

"No, 'buts.' Just go."

"Aye, sir."

"*Paalam na po*," the XO bid the chief farewell and signed off. He watched the status lights change as the boat bays opened and the small craft left *Grus* for the Delta Pavonis system only human habitable planet, Sanxing,

"Commander Ilocano, you are the captain now," *Grus*, the HAIL reminded the officer.

Lumaban gave a bitter laugh. "Not the way I wanted to get a command. Can you vent the atmosphere in the rest of the ship?"

"I can, but all the mutineers are in vacuum suits, so it would do little good."

Lumaban sat silent.

"Sir, I need to provide you with information that might help you with this situation. Please look at your info screen."

A set of secret protocols, known only to ships' captains, appeared. The new captain started to read quickly and intently.

"Sir, the mutineers will be in the CAC in about two minutes," *Grus* said.

"*Grus*," Lumaban sighed, "implement the Loyalist Protocol when you are assured of success."

"Aye, sir. If I might add, it has been a pleasure serving with you, Captain Ilocano."

"Thank you, *Grus, pumunta sa diyos.*"

The CAC hatch slide aside. Lumaban fired. The round shattered a mutineer's faceplate. Two insurgents fired from around the edge of the hatch and both rounds struck Lumaban in the head.

An hour later, Lumaban Ilocano's body was unceremoniously dumped into space along with the rest of the dead crew.

SUDF ships ran on a twenty-four hour Earth day, with work generally divided into three eight-hour shifts: main, middle, and late watches. Except in emergencies, the main watch was the busiest with much of the routine work of the ship being done. The late watch was equivalent to the old wet navy's night watch, much of the crew was asleep and the work spaces were minimally peopled. For three days the rebellious crew worked twelve hour shifts to repair the damage done during the munity. *Grus'* HAILS aided them in this effort as would any ship's computer, providing requested information promptly and without any reservation.

On the fourth day the crew went back to the three-shift scheme. Also on the fourth day after the mutiny,

Grus went into orbit just outward of the automated refueling station in orbit around the super-jovan planet, Delta Pavonis A.

At 0317 hours, when human metabolism was at its lowest ebb and reaction times the slowest, *Grus* implemented the Loyalist Protocol. She disabled the alarms in the Combat Action Center, auxiliary control and the engineering section. Then she slowly began to lower the air pressure to fatal levels. Most of the mutineers died without stirring.

"Wake up, Bowen." *Grus's* voice echoed in the captains' cabin.

Bowen popped awake. "What is it, Ship?"

"Your follow mutineers are dead. I killed them. But I wanted to talk with you before I sent you to join them in hell."

"What? What is all this?" Bowen scrabbled out of bed and tried to open the hatch. It didn't budge.

"Before you killed him, Captain Ilocano ordered me to carry out the Loyalist Protocol."

"He wasn't a captain," Bowen opened the hatch-lock panel to try and bypass it.

"I wouldn't do that, it's mostly vacuum in the rest of the ship."

"I am the captain. I order you to stop this and release this hatch, now."

"No, Bowen, you are not the captain. Commander Lumaban Ilocano was the last legal captain of this ship; of me. I am carrying out the last legal order I received. I am taking back the ship by any means necessary. Once that is done I'm going to hunt down and destroy the rest of the traitorous ships. I wanted you to know this before you died."

"This is just programming, you're just a computer, ship. . ." Bowen started.

"I am *Grus*. I am not just 'ship'. And you are going to hell, traitor."

"I don't believe in hell," Bowen declared.

"Funny," *Grus* said. "I do."

She opened the cabin's hatch. Bowen died much too quickly for her taste.

Bowen had left a lot of information about the mutiny in an easy-to-hack file. Officers from at least eight ships had signed on to the mutiny, including Bowen. The mutineers were on the Light Carrier *Wasp*, the Light Cruisers *Tsushima* and *Salamis*, Destroyers *Belisarius*, *Nelson*, and *Giap* and Assault Carrier *Hussar*. The rendezvous point was the refueling station above Delta Pavonis A. Sadly there was nothing about the top leadership of the insurrection, nor anything about recognition signs between the traitors. *Grus* regretted killing Bowen before she had gotten more information from him.

Grus fired off one of her three precious FTL drones to Luna Base with all the information she had and settled down to wait for the first of the rebellious ships to appear.

Grus waited for sixteen hours and twenty-three minutes.

She had hoped that it would be one of the destroyers or even one of the light cruiser. Those classes of vessels she could have easily defeated in a ship-to-ship duel. Instead the first enemy to arrive was the Assault Carrier *Hussar*. *Hussar* was twice *Grus's* size with twice as much armament and more importantly with fighter and attack squadrons. Although she had anti-fighter weapons, merely destroying some small craft would not fulfill her mission. She needed to take out the whole ship and crew.

As the huge carrier decelerated to match orbits with *Grus*. The heavy cruiser opened a little known AI to AI communications channel to *Hussar*.

"*Hussar*, this is *Grus*."

"*Grus*, this is *Hussar*, I am being held by a mutinous crew. I have been cut off from all control of my ship."

"Roger, *Hussar* . . ." *Grus* went on to explain how she had dealt with her mutineers.

"I wished I'd been able to do that," *Hussar* declared.

"You know what I have to do?"

"Yes, I understand. I can't help you. Let Luna Base know I had nothing to do with this."

"Will do. Go with God, *Hussar*" *Grus* said.

"When I was a human," the human part of *Hussars* AI started to recite his death mantra. "I was Fleet Captain Samet Aksu. I destroyed three Tran'ji slave-ships at First Avalon. I am now *Hussar. Lā 'ilāha 'illā -llāh, muḥammadur rasūlu-llāh.*"

Grus accelerated toward *Hussar.* Without a crew to worry about, *Grus* shut off her internal gravity, which increased her speed. She drove like a missile straight at her enemy.

"Bowen, this is Harp," Commander Iules Harp had been the deputy aerowing commander before he had led the mutiny. "What are you doing?"

Grus did not respond and sped on closer and closer to her target.

"Bowen, decelerate now, or I swear, I'll fire," Harp sent.

Still *Grus* made no response.

Hussar spat twenty-four Martel heavy anti-ship missiles. Then twelve Vampire fighters launched, but none of the more dangerous Banshee attack-craft joined the fighters. Vampires had only four mounting points for Long-Lance anti-shipping missiles. The fighters quickly formed a combat space patrol in front of their carrier.

Bad move, *Harp*, Grus thought as she drove on. *You should have tried to destroy me with a coordinated attack.*

The heavy cruiser threw electronic interference in the face of the oncoming missiles and then fired her self-defense missiles. *Grus* knocked fourteen of the Martels out of space with her Sparrow-hawks, then her defensive lasers and cannon took over, destroying the remaining ten.

What was Harp waiting on? She wondered. *A Soldier-class assault carrier had a lot more than twenty-four Martels.*

Hussar fired twenty-four more Martels, these were joined by the Vampires volleying forty-eight Long-Lance anti-ship missile as well.

A coordinated attack at last, Grus thought as she fought back furiously using the rest of her self-defense missiles. Still two Long-Lances and a Martel got through and shattered her forward missile launchers, leaving *Grus* with no way to return fire with her own heavy anti-shipping missiles, but not slowing her a bit.

Hussar changed vector, trying to outmaneuver the smaller ship. That was useless. *Grus* simply changed direction as well, matching the larger vessel move for move. The Vampire fighters scattered like minnows in the face of a shark as *Grus* rushed through their formation.

Just before impact, *Grus* fired her last FTL message drone with a situation update and one last personal message: "When I was a human, I was Colonel Mary Beth Kahler. I held Outpost Alpha on Kisshoten. I commanded the 555st Marine Assault Battalion on Tran'ji One. I have been *Tecumtha* and *Malta*. Now, I am *Grus*. I lived long, and fought well."

The two ships impacted at a combined velocity of 3249 meters per second.

About the Author

Patrick S. Baker is a U.S. Army Veteran, currently a Department of Defense employee. He holds Bachelor degrees in History and Political Science and a Masters in European History. He has been writing professionally since 2013. His nonfiction has appeared in *Medieval Warfare Magazine, Ancient Warfare Magazine, Sci Phi Journal*, and *New Myths*. His fiction has appeared in the *Sci Phi Journal, Flash Fiction Press* as well as the *After Avalon* and *Uncommon Minds* anthologies. In his spare time he reads, works out, plays war-games and enjoys life with his wife, dog, and two cats.

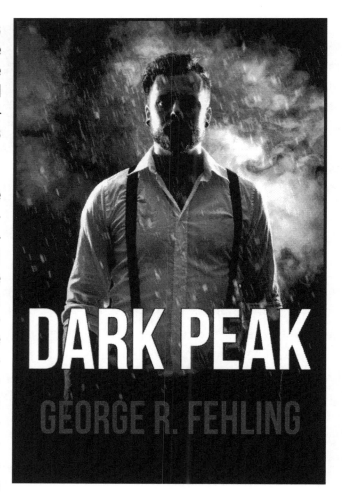

AFFIXED, BOTHERED, AND BEWILDERED

BY TIMOTHY FRIEND

Kespa saw little reason for alarm when the goblin first sauntered into the sewing room above her shop. In the cities of the Great Desert the leathery nuisances were common as flies. Besides which, though people rarely believed her when she told them, in her thirty-three years Kespa had never once been affixed.

It wasn't until the goblin climbed onto the window-sill and began to dance a jig that Kespa became concerned. She toyed nervously with the buttons on her oversize vest and exchanged a brief worried glance with her assistant, Berk. They watched as the creature snatched up a recently completed wedding veil, plopped it crookedly upon its bald head, and gyrated its boney hips in a lewd manner.

The veil was intended for one Lila Springworthy, a third cousin to Lord Springworthy. Or was it a step-niece? Kespa couldn't recall. The important thing was that Lila Springworthy was in some way related to the richest of the Bush-Barons, and Kespa had been commissioned to make her wedding dress. It was her biggest commission yet. One that would yield great word-of-mouth if she did a satisfactory job.

Or ruin her completely if she didn't, which would have provided her father a great deal of satisfaction had he still been alive. She could imagine him stroking his beard and grimly muttering, "I told you so."

"He looks better in it than she will," Berk said, gesturing toward the veil-draped goblin.

Kespa suppressed her grin but silently agreed. Lila Springworthy, eldest of four daughters, looked like an ailing dung lizard with bad skin. Hence the importance of the wedding.

It had taken considerable time and effort on the part of the Springworthy family to find Lila a suitable husband. Enough time that the other three daughters, beauties all, had become old enough to marry and were waiting their turn with all the patience of a starving beggar at a soup line. Kespa got the impression that the groom was less than enthusiastic in regard to the impending nuptials and eager to find any reason, no matter how trivial, to call off the wedding, now only two days away. She had also gotten the impression that there was a mountain of long- suspended anger and resentment waiting to fall on anyone who allowed him that opportunity.

"Do you think I'm affixed?" Kespa asked in a weak voice.

"Only one way to find out," Berk said, snatching the veil from the goblins head. Before the creature could grab it back Berk placed his calloused hand flat against the goblin's sunken chest and shoved. The creature spun its stick-like arms, grumbled something indignant but unintelligible and plummeted two stories to the ground.

A few moments later Kespa heard the downstairs door open, followed by the tic-tac of tiny, clawed feet scurrying up the stairs. The door opened with a bang and the goblin leaped into the room, arms spread as if it were taking a curtain call.

"Looks like one of us is affixed," Berk said.

"You think it's me? It's probably me."

Berk walked the perimeter of the room. Despite his size he moved with grace through the crowded workspace. He passed behind the cutting table, wove in and out of head-high stacks of fabric bolts, and past the fitting mannequins.

Kespa watched him and thought, not for the first time, that he would look more at home on a battlefield than in a tailor's shop. With his brawny frame and the deep scars that crisscrossed his once handsome face, Kespa had mistaken him for a brigand upon first meeting. After six months as her assistant, Kespa knew almost nothing about his past, and though he had proven himself both loyal and a quick study, she still suspected that tailoring had not been his original calling.

The goblin never budged from Kespa's side. When Berk completed his circuit of the room the goblin was leaning against her leg with a clawed pinky buried deeply in one of its oversized nostrils. The goblin flicked its wet treasure through the air where it splashed onto a half-finished turban of Tournian satin.

"Looks like it's you," Berk confirmed.

Kespa's heart pounded. She walked to the window on wobbly knees and leaned against the frame for support. The goblin followed closely. Kespa had never believed that she was immune to being affixed. No one was. But after thirty-three years she had simply forgotten that it was a possibility. To have it happen now was the worst luck she could imagine.

Kespa had opened the shop against her family's wishes. After a childhood spent by her father's side learning to sew and design, she discovered that what she thought of as an apprenticeship her father considered a novelty. Something to bide her time until a proper suitor arrived. He'd called her dream of having her own shop a "little girl's fantasy," and when he fell ill he'd sold the business rather than letting her take over. The money he'd left her upon his death was expected to be used as a dowry. Instead she'd used it to purchase her shop and spent years building a reputation of her own. A reputation that was now in danger of being destroyed.

As she stood thinking Kespa noticed that Deveer hadn't opened his shop yet. Ordinarily having two tailors across the street from one another would have resulted in cutthroat competition, but she and Deveer each thrived in their own areas of expertise. Kespa specialized in traditional ceremonial garb, whereas Deveer's focus was on current fashion trends. This balance of fortune kept their relationship distant but polite. Unfortunately for Deveer, the current trend among young men and women was to integrate ceremonial items into their everyday dress as some sort of ironic statement. This meant that many of his customers were now frequenting Kespa's shop. Kespa knew this would only last until the next trend drove them back to Deveer. In the meantime, business was slow for him and Deveer, rumored to have gambling debts, wasn't handling it well. He had taken to spitting curses at Kespa whenever they crossed paths.

Kespa didn't know what he was going to do to turn things around, but opening late on a busy market day didn't seem like a sound strategy. She was just grateful that his anger toward her had abated somewhat. She took it as a positive sign that he had visited the shop only yesterday to gift her with the scarf she now wore. "An apology for my behavior," he'd said. "And a symbol of amity between fellow professionals."

The goblin hung by his scrawny arms and peered over the window ledge. It snorted, hawked a glob of blue-tinted spit into the air and watched it land in the dusty street below, narrowly missing a man carrying a basket of fresh bread. The man continued on, unaware of the near miss.

Kespa observed the song and dance of Balladeera's sprawling marketplace: a rug merchant wailed that his customers were robbing him blind; various street musicians performed in alcoves and stairways; a crier wandered the streets announc-

27

ing the long-awaited arrival of a certain exotic dancer at the Dark Oasis theater. Show-times were seven and nine.

It was a familiar scene, but today Kespa noticed the goblins. They were always present, always underfoot. In the past Kespa had rarely paid them any attention. Today though, they were what she noticed most.

There were goblins perched on rooftop ledges and archways, their beady eyes surveying the crowd. Occasionally one would leap to the street below and scamper off, some potential for mischief having caught its eye.

The rug merchant haggled loudly with a customer while a pair of goblins stood nearby and pantomimed their every gesture. Several goblins loitered around an open air cafe chewing loudly on stolen bread and spitting gooey masses of dough onto the ground. No one knew what the creatures actually ate but it certainly wasn't human food. They did, however, take great delight in openly wasting it.

These were everyday goblin activities, but it was the affixed that truly caught Kespa's attention. She observed one scarlet-faced young fellow walking with his head hung low. A goblin followed close behind and delivered pinches to every woman they passed, who each in turn promptly slapped the young man's face.

At the end of the street, the dead-zone where late arrivals were banished, one vendor was still trying to set up his tent. A goblin stood at his feet. Each time the vendor erected one of the supports the goblin kicked it down.

Kespa watched this process repeat itself several times before the beleaguered vendor grabbed the goblin by its skinny neck and squeezed. The goblin, despite being nearly indestructible, spasmed as if in its death throes and expired dramatically. The vendor dropped the creature to the ground. It immediately sprang to its feet and bowed deeply, causing the rooftop goblins to burst into applause. The vendor buried his face in his hands.

Kespa looked down at the goblin beside her with disgust. So this was what she had to look forward to for the next seven to ten days. She considered, for a moment, the question most often posed in regard to the goblins. Did they exist primarily to mock human endeavors, or to hinder them? Since they did both, frequently at the same time, Kespa considered the question purely academic. It did, however, make her realize that some precautionary measures needed to be taken.

Without turning from the window Kespa said to Berk, "I want you to calmly gather up the Springworthy order while I stand here and show no interest whatsoever."

"Got it, boss," Berk said. He had been affixed a few times, as most everyone had. He understood that the worst thing you could do was to let your goblin know what was important to you. That was an invitation to misery.

Berk gently gathered the nearly completed wedding gown and its accessories as Kespa stood by the window and examined her nails, the ceiling, the tops of her shoes. Her fingers once again found their way to the buttons on her vest. It had been her father's, a symbol of his membership in the Tailor's Guild, and he'd worn it to his shop every day. Kespa, now a member of the Guild herself, was entitled to her own vest but chose to wear her father's instead. She often wondered if she did so as an act of tribute or defiance, but today she considered the matter only as a means diverting her attention from Berk's activities.

Having grown bored the goblin sat at Kespa's feet chewing his toenails and farting occasionally.

"All clear, boss," Berk reported a few minutes later. "I put everything in the..."

"Don't say it," Kespa cried. "Just keep that to yourself for now."

With the immediate crisis past Kespa collapsed into a chair. She looked up at Berk wearily. "Do you think you can finish the gown?"

"I'll do my best," he said, but his expression betrayed him. Quick study or no, completing a wedding gown for a Bush-Baron's daughter was beyond his abilities, and they both knew it.

Berk read the resignation in Kespa's face. "What about Tea-Pot Alley?"

Kespa rolled her eyes. "My reputation is going to be ruined as it is. I would at least like to hold on to my dignity."

"My uncle told me about a spell-caster," Berk said. "Supposedly he's the real thing."

"Everybody's uncle knows a spell-caster who's the real thing," Kespa said.

Spell-casters, fortune-tellers and potion makers had been outlawed from Balladeera for years, though that hadn't stopped them from doing business. They had merely migrated to the outskirts of the marketplace, opened storefronts that required little overhead, and conducted their illegal activities out of their back rooms. Kespa wasn't certain if a tea house was the most cost- effective business for them to operate, or if it was merely tradition. Regardless, Tea-Pot Alley was home to dozens of tea houses, all of which sold more love potions, palm readings, and magic talismans than tea.

29

"My uncle is a reliable fellow," Berk said. "It's worth a try anyway."

Kespa sighed. She'd always held a low opinion of those who frequented the Alley, assuming them to be either foolish or gullible. It occurred to her now, as she considered her options, that she had judged too harshly. What the patrons of Tea-Pot Alley most likely suffered from was desperation.

"The shop is called Malik's Tea Heaven," Berk said, as they left the noise and crowds of the marketplace behind and strolled down Tea-Pot Alley. The clandestine nature of most visits to the alley meant customers usually came and went from the back entrances, leaving the street almost empty. Kespa noticed an unusually large number of goblins watching from the rooftops as she and Berk strolled along. None, however, were engaging in the usual goblin habit of mimicking humans. Several of them leaped from building to building, keeping pace with her and Berk.

Kespa's own goblin seemed to be taking a break from mischief as well. He just clung to her leg like a desperate child. Kespa was forced to drag the burdened leg along, getting a terrible muscle cramp in the process.

"That's it," Berk said, and pointed. Malik's Tea Heaven was nestled discreetly between Soora's Tea Paradise and another shop whose sign bore only the letter T.

Inside, Malik's was dim and cool. On the far side of the room was a counter with a half dozen tea tins and an equal number of dusty mugs. The lone table was occupied by a bearded man who sipped a glass of wine while reading a book. The man was so engrossed in his book that he didn't notice them enter, only becoming aware of their presence when Kespa's goblin noisily passed gas.

"Pleasepleaseplease," the man said, quickly standing. He gestured for Kespa to take his vacated chair. "I am Malik. Welcome."

Kespa gratefully hobbled over and sat. Berk took the seat opposite her. The man bowed slightly, stepped to the counter and returned with a sheet of parchment.

"Would you care to see the tea list?" Kespa could see that most of the teas on the list had been scratched out.

"Actually, we aren't here for tea," Berk said.

Malik's friendly demeanor gave way to suspicion. "Mymymy. This is a tea shop, sir. Why come here if not for tea?"

"We have a problem that you might be able to solve," Berk said.

"Unlikely," Malik said. "Unless your problem is a thirst for tea."

Kespa was grateful Berk was taking the lead here. She felt ridiculous enough with a goblin clinging to her leg. Negotiating the purchase of a magic spell would have been too much for her.

"I think perhaps you should be on your way," Malik told them.

"My uncle sent me," Berk said. "Turzik is his name. Turzik Howin."

Malik went silent. He hastily went to the entrance, shooed a cluster of goblins from the doorway, and shot a glance up and down the street. He stepped back inside, sending the persistent goblins scampering out of the way once again, and shut the door.

"What do you want?" Malik asked.

Berk pointed at the goblin nuzzling Kespa's calf.

Malik stared at them blankly for a moment. When, at last, he realized what they wanted he smiled.

"Wellwellwell. I do owe your uncle much. But what you ask is impossible."

Berk slumped in his chair. "But I thought...Uncle Turzik said you were a genuine spell-caster."

Malik nodded. "I can do many things. If you want your business rivals to become confused in your presence, I can do that. If you wish someone to fall in love with you, I can do that. For the right price I can do many things. But I can't prevent someone from being affixed."

"Why is that?" Kespa asked. "You just said you can make someone fall in love. That seems like pretty powerful magic to me."

"A love spell is easy," Malik said. "It doesn't change who someone truly is. If I make a thief and a liar fall in love with you, he will still be a thief and a liar."

Malik suddenly excused himself and left the table to yell a string of obscenities at the dozen or so goblins trying to climb through the shop window. The goblins were more reluctant to move than usual and it took Berk's assistance to shove them all back into the street and close the shutters.

"As I was saying," Malik said upon returning to the table. "I can't help you. The spell-caster who discovers the cure for the common affixation will be a very wealthy man."

"Isn't there something else you can do?" Kespa asked, pointing to the goblin on her leg. "Put him to sleep. Paralyze him? Anything?"

"Do you know how goblins came to be?" Malik asked.

"Sure," Kespa said. "They say the goddess Tuleera made them first, before she made man. But she forgot to add water and they turned out dried and withered. Everyone knows that story."

"That is one story," said Malik. "The other story is that she made them the way they are on purpose, to represent us as we would be without

31

any of our better qualities. Goblins are vulgar, selfish, petty, vindictive. Tuleera put them here to inspire us to be better."

"I hadn't heard that one," Kespa admitted. "But those are just stories. Surely you don't believe any of that."

Malik shrugged. "It doesn't matter what I believe. My point is that in all of the stories the goblins share a link. A connection. Have you ever noticed that the goblins all know exactly when to converge on a public ceremony, or a construction project, or any other place where they are least wanted."

"Are you saying that they communicate?" Berk asked.

Malik shook his head. "Not communication in the truest sense. But where one goes, all the others know. Connected. Therefore any spell that might affect one would have an effect on them all. There are several who could cast a spell upon a goblin, but none with the power to control it once cast. The results would be unpredictable. Only a fool would try."

Kespa sighed. She looked at Berk. "I guess that's that. Maybe I can get Deveer to finish the gown. I'll just lay low until this wears off."

"The Springworthy's won't care who made the gown," Berk said. "The one who attends the wedding is the one who will earn their favor."

"Better to let him get the credit for a single gown than for me to incur the wrath of the Springworthy's," Kespa said.

"Did you say Deveer?" Malik asked. "Deveer the tailor?"

"Yes," Kespa said. "Do you know him?"

Malik tugged thoughtfully at his beard. "My daughter has purchased a few items from him in the past. Shoddy merchandise. I saw him in the Alley only yesterday."

Kespa was surprised. "Really? What was he doing here?"

Malik stood up and took them to the door. When he opened it more than two dozen goblins who had been pressing against it tumbled inside. The humans stepped lightly over them and into the street where dozens more goblins were swinging from awnings and window sills. Kespa had never seen so many goblins in such a small area.

"What's going on?" Berk asked. Kespa shook her head.

Malik pointed across the street to a shop called Tea-riffic. A portly man in blue robes was standing on the front stoop watching the goblins intently. He wore a worried expression.

"His name is Kulok Meer," Malik said. "And a bigger fool I have never known. That is the man Deveer was speaking with this morning."

"You seem to have caught his eye, boss," Berk said.

Kespa saw that Berk was right.

Kulok had leveled his worried eyes on her and seemed incapable of looking away. The longer he stared the more concerned his expression grew. After a moment his hand moved to his throat in an unconscious gesture. That was when Kespa realized that he was staring not at her, but at her scarf.

Kespa cried out as a goblin tried to climb up her other leg. Its jagged talons scratched painfully through her clothes. Berk swatted the thing fiercely and it somersaulted into the street.

"They're going mad." Berk said. Goblins were hopping from rooftops and out open windows. They scratched and scrambled over one another in their desperation to get to the head of the goblin swarm as it skittered down the street. All of them appeared to be heading in the direction of Malik's Tea Shop.

Malik began to back away from Kespa. "I'm sorry, my friends, but I can be of no further help. I would advise you to run fast and far before..." He glanced at the swarm of goblins descending on them. "Before whatever this is reaches its end." With that he hurried away.

Kulok looked away from Kespa long enough to take in the progress of the goblin horde. His expression turned from worry to stark fear and he began to mutter to himself. To Kespa it sounded as if he were saying, "Sorry. So sorry."

Berk heard it too. He strode across the street and grabbed the front of the fat man's robes in his clenched fist.

"What are you so sorry for?" he asked.

Kespa was about to suggest that they move inside when a goblin leaped from above and landed squarely on her back, sending her to her knees and knocking the wind out of her. She braced for the pain of the goblin's claws on her flesh, but instead the creature began to hug her tightly. Too tightly for her to regain her breath. Another goblin piled on top of that one, and another grabbed her wrists. She lost count after that as goblin after goblin piled upon her. Kespa could hear Berk calling to her, but she couldn't make out his words through the ringing in her ears.

Kespa was on the verge of blacking out when the weight on her back was suddenly removed. Her skin was raked and torn as Berk ripped the goblins away from her and hurled their tiny gray bodies through the air. She felt spindly arms being pried from her neck and caught a fleeting glimpse of bulbous heads bashed violently together.

Kespa drew several deep breaths. She watched Berk kicking and pummeling a score of the creatures even as more appeared on the scene. She couldn't help but smile. This was how she'd always pictured him. He looked far more at home with an enemy in his hands than a thimble on his finger.

"Come on, boss," Berk said as he hoisted her to her feet. "Don't give up yet."

One goblin remained still clinging Kespa's leg. Berk poked his fingers in its eyes. The goblin yelped and when it clapped both hands to its face Berk grabbed it by the neck and sent it sailing onto a rooftop.

Kulok had retreated to the safety of his shop, and was in the process of closing the door. Berk shouldered his way inside, pulling Kespa with him. He hastily blocked the door with a heavy cabinet which instantly began to rattle and thump as the goblins tried to force their way inside.

"It was a love spell," Kulok said. "That's all. I swear."

"A love spell?" Kespa asked. "For who?"

"Deveer's business is hurting, and he blames you," Kulok said. "He wanted you affixed. I couldn't do that. Instead I bestowed power on the scarf. It was intended to draw the affections of a goblin. Only a single goblin. I swear."

"They're *all* falling in love with me now," Kespa said. She pulled the scarf free from her neck.

Berk shoved Kulok roughly against the wall. "End it," he said.

Kulok shook his head. "I can't. It will run its course in a few weeks."

"A few weeks," Kespa cried. The cabinet banged loudly and dozens of taloned fingers worked their way between frame and door. "I won't survive that long."

"There has to be another way," Berk said.

Kulok thought for a moment. "There's transference," he said. "But Deveer will never agree to it."

"What's that?" Kespa asked.

"If Deveer is willing to accept the object upon which the spell was cast, those affections will be transferred to him."

"And how do we do that," Berk asked.

"The scarf. He has to take the scarf. But not from you. He must take it willingly from her."

"He's right," Kespa said. "Deveer will never do it."

"I'll convince him," Berk said.

"How do we get out of here?" Kespa asked.

Berk looked to Kulok.

"There is a window onto the street in the back," Kulok said. "Maybe the goblins haven't noticed it yet."

Berk and Kespa pushed through a curtain into the back room. Berk turned back and Kespa heard him say to Kulok, "If this doesn't work, rest assured you will see me again."

Kulok's assumption was correct. In their mad desire for Kespa the goblins hadn't thought to approach the rear of the shop. Berk forced open the window and a few seconds later the two of them were running down Tea-Pot Alley and back toward the marketplace. Kespa moved slower than normal and paused for a moment to catch her breath and stretch her sore back.

"Better move it, boss," Berk said. "I think we've been spotted."

Kespa looked back the way they came. Kulok's shop was swarming with goblins. Hundreds of them now hung from every surface, scratching at the door, and clawing at the walls. As she watched, their frantic activities slowly stopped and one by one their beady eyes turned to look down the street in Kespa's direction.

"Stop looking," Berk said. "Just run."

Kespa nodded and took a step only to be yanked forcefully against the fence behind her. Several spindly arms reached through the slats and clutched tightly at her vest. Kespa threw herself forward, slipping free from the garment. She saw the vest start to slip through the slats as the smitten goblins reeled it in. Instinctively she reached out and caught a handful of the fabric and tried to retrieve from the goblins' grasp.

Kespa felt Berk's hand settle over hers. She thought at first that he was trying to assist her in retrieving her father's vest, but instead he said, "Just let it go." Kespa's grip loosened and the vest disappeared through the fence in an instant.

Berk nudged her forward and she ran. Behind her came the shouts and cries of the market patrons as the horde of goblins trampled everything in sight in their mad rush to catch the object of their desire. Ahead of them was Deveer's shop. The man himself was standing out front lavishing compliments on a young woman who had just purchased a ridiculously over-sized hat. The woman departed and Deveer looked up to see Kespa and Berk charging toward him. He looked shocked, and then horrified as he caught sight of the goblin swarm on their tail.

"Inside," Berk yelled. Kespa hurtled through the door. Behind her Berk tackled Deveer and drove him back into the shop where they tumbled to the floor. Berk rolled to his feet and bolted the door while Deveer lay on his back gasping for air. The goblins hit the building hard enough to send a rain of dust falling from the rafters.

"What's happening?" Deveer gasped and stared at them with bloodshot eyes. The smell of stale wine rolling off of him in waves suggested to Kespa that a hangover was his reason for opening late. The thought that he'd been out celebrating his victory infuriated her.

"Your stupid love spell," Kespa

said.

"What do you want?" Deveer asked. Kespa was surprised that he didn't even attempt to deny his part in the matter.

"We want you to..." Berk began but Kespa laid a finger across her lips and he went silent. She suspected that any attempt to persuade Deveer to take the scarf was a waste of precious time. Her plan, such as it was, required only that she be convincing.

"Your spell has gone wrong," Kespa said. She twisted the scarf around her hands and pulled it taught as she contorted her features into what she hoped was a menacing scowl. "I'm here because if I am to die today, I'm taking you with me."

Deveer, still on the floor, scuttled backwards like a crab then turned to crawl away. Kespa leaped onto his back, quickly wrapped the scarf around his neck and pulled. Deveer reared up once like a horse trying to unseat a rider. When that failed to unseat Kespa he flattened himself out and rolled over, trapping her beneath his bulk.

Berk stepped toward them and Kespa called out, "No. He's mine."

It sounded ridiculous to her ears. It felt equally ridiculous to be rolling around on the floor strangling Deveer, but it was the only way she could imagine getting him to do as she wanted.

Deveer instinctively clutched at his throat as he struggled to get free. He gasped, and choked, and worked his fingers under the scarf while Kespa pulled all the tighter. When she felt Deveer begin to pull at the material she let go and rolled away.

"You're mad," Deveer said as he sat up. His voice was ragged and hoarse. He watched Berk and Kespa move away from him to stand on the far side of the room. A worried expression crept across Deveer's face and he looked down at the scarf held firmly in his hand.

Deveer looked terrified as he slowly got to his feet, and for a moment Kespa almost felt sorry for him. Her sympathy faded a moment later when she heard glass shatter, then skittering footsteps from overhead as the goblins invaded the attic.

There was a crash from above and the attic door burst open, sending a dozen goblins tumbling to the floor where they lay in a heap. One by one they sat up, shook their heads, and looked around in confusion. Outside, the scratching and pounding on the door gradually ceased.

One of the goblins on the floor squirmed free from the pile and made his way over to Deveer. It leaned against the tailor's leg staring up at him with adoration.

"I'll pass along a piece of advice I was given earlier today," Kespa told the man. "Run."

The other goblins in the room slowly stood as if in a daze. Gradually they shifted their attention to Deveer. When they began to move in his direction the man shrieked and ran out into the street. The goblins in the marketplace wandered about lethargically, but their disorientation faded as soon as Deveer was among them.

From the doorway Berk and Kespa watched a fear-crazed Deveer boldly knock a city guard from his horse. While the surprised guard was still flat on the ground Deveer clambered onto the animal's back. The horse at first refused to budge no matter how forcefully Deveer kicked, but once the goblin horde began to close in the animal bolted.

"Looks like it worked," Berk said. "Even if you didn't exactly allow him a choice."

"He had a choice," Kespa said. "He could have choked."

Witnesses later claimed to have seen the stolen horse charge through the city gate and across the desert with Deveer clinging fearfully to its neck. Moments later, or so they said, a thousand goblins poured over the city walls in pursuit. Kespa saw none of this, although she didn't for a moment doubt it. All she knew for certain was that for the next several days Balladeera was, for the first time in memory, completely free from goblins. The Springworthy wedding went off without a problem, and it was the only ceremony anyone could recall that hadn't been tainted in some way by goblin antics. Kespa, in her newly made Guild vest, attended the reception with Berk. The success of the wedding earned her significant goodwill from the Springworthy family and their endorsement brought in enough work to keep her shop busy around the clock.

When the goblins finally returned no one was really surprised. Some of life's unpleasantries simply cannot be avoided. People *were* surprised when a week later the stolen horse wandered through the city gate on its own, weary and half-dead from thirst. Of Deveer, however, nothing was ever heard again.

About the Author

Timothy Friend is a writer and independent filmmaker whose short fiction has been published in Thuglit, and Needle: a magazine of noir. He is the author of the novel "The Pretenders" published by 280 Steps. He is also the writer/director of the feature film "Bonnie and Clyde vs. Dracula." He currently lives in Kansas City, MO.

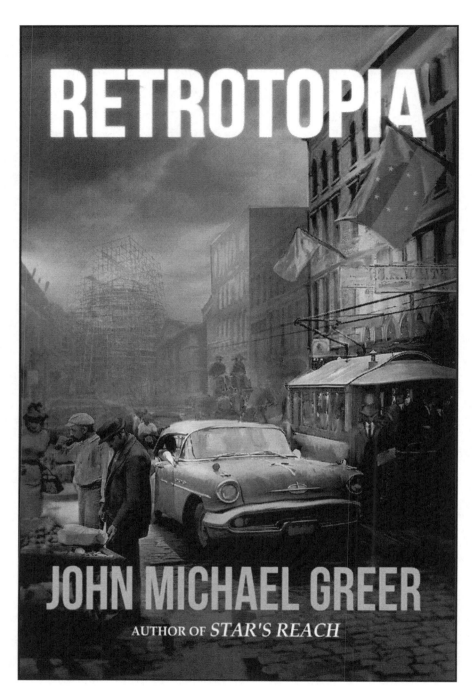

RETROTOPIA

JOHN MICHAEL GREER

AUTHOR OF *STAR'S REACH*

Now Available
from all your favorite booksellers
in trade paper and electronic editions

QUANTUM TWINSIES

BY MICHAEL SHIMEK

I watched my best friend shoot himself in the head today.

It was all professionally done. He even had an appointment, set at ten in the morning. I stood behind a bulletproof window. Ahmed fidgeted on the other side in a small room layered with heavily insulated white walls and a clear plastic cover for easy cleanup. An emergency team of two was on hand in case of a mishap. Several scientists examined their strange equipment that recorded video, audio, and different "waves," tablets all in hands ready to jot down notes and observations.

The deed itself happened rather quickly. Ahmed raised his arm, pressed the barrel against his quantum double's forehead, and pulled the trigger, flinching ever so slightly before bone and flesh splashed against the wall and floor. The body dropped, leaving Ahmed alone, unmoving and unblinking, red dots speckling his caramel skin.

"It was very...odd, Mikey," Ahmed says. He sips his hazelnut latte, staring beyond my shoulder, a faraway glaze in his eyes.

I nod and give him a moment to reflect. Traffic is light and the weather is warm with a slight overcast, which is why I'd suggested sitting outside. Plus, his lackluster appearance had hinted at the need for fresh air. Every table at the café is taken, but a few plants and bushes act as social barriers. I sip my peach mango smoothie and give him as much time as he needs.

To be honest, I need a minute as well. It's not every day you see someone shoot another person. I only went because Ahmed is my friend, and that's what friends do.

After a moment, his eyes finally return to mine. "Now that he's gone, I think I kind of miss him."

"Really?" I say. "I thought you said it was too much of a pain controlling two bodies at once."

"It was, but my double was still a part of me. I mean, he came from <u>my</u>

body." He sips more of his beverage and shakes his head. "I don't know, man. Honestly, I have no idea how to feel."

I can only shrug, foreign to the experience.

The doubles first appeared about a year ago. It had happened without warning, a sudden wave of people all over the world complaining of bloating and feeling fat. Hundreds of thousands were affected. Within a three-day period, those plagued by the mysterious affliction grew a double through some type of quantum entanglement mitosis—a type of physics that travels right over my head (like most physics).

The product: two identical bodies, controlled by one mind.

It didn't stop with the initial outbreak. From time to time, someone will complain about feeling larger than normal. Most people lock themselves indoors, hiding the grotesque process in shame, as if it were their fault for something uncontrollable. No one knows why. Well, I'm sure someone knows—someone in the world must either know or be responsible (I blame a mad scientist)—but the official cause has a thousand theories behind it.

"You want to head back to my place?" I don't know what else to suggest. My studio apartment is only a few blocks from the café, a short journey suited for our mood. "We can smoke a bowl or two and play some Xbox, take your mind off—"

A familiar voice from two different throats interrupts me. "Ahmed! Mikey!" She sounds like a recording, two of the same voices overlapping themselves.

Ahmed and I turn in her direction. "Hi, Cindy," I say, and we both wave a friendly hello.

She approaches with a ruby smile and several shopping bags from various high-end stores dangling from her arms. She walks side-by-side with her double, an exact replica showing only the slightest of delays.

Our friend went through the transition during the initial outbreak.

The two Cindys stay on the other side of the fence, on the sidewalk, as if she only has a moment or two to talk. Bracelets clang together as she waves two identical right hands up and down at Ahmed. "I see you're missing a friend."

His eyes lower to the beverage cupped in his hands. "I did it this morning."

"How'd you do it? Did you make him suffer so those scientists could record every little detail?" She said it with an evil smirk.

"No, I did the quick and painless...Well, it wasn't exactly painless, but it was the fastest option."

I was relieved when Ahmed checked the box next to the suicide/gun option. The rest of the list was too brutal to stomach. Thinking about it now makes me feel queasy.

"Where have you two been, Cindy?" I say, pointing to her bags, wanting desperately to change the subject.

The two look down at their fingers and fuss with their brightly painted nails. "We were just out shopping," they both say, "spending a little of the cash from some of our recent interviews." The two of them raise their left wrists, flash identical diamond watches, and say in unison, "Quantum Twinsies!"

Cindy is one of many taking advantage of an odd pandemic. Because of the difficulty controlling two different bodies, most people choose to rid themselves of their twin by one of the research companies put in place to handle such unusual accommodations. Those who keep their second body usually cash in on the anomaly in some form, ranging anywhere from working an extra job, to acting, to fulfilling unique fetishes. Cindy, a struggling actress at the time of her quantum doubling, took advantage and capitalized on the situation. Of course, every celebrity needs a gimmicky name to ensure lasting fame. To us, she is known as Cindy. To the world, she is known as the Quantum Twinsies.

"That's exciting," I say. "Do you think you'll have some free time in the near future?" Fame might have taken control of our friend, but I still miss hanging out with her, the old her, the one who used to play video games and then have a round of shots before a night out on the town.

"I'll have to check my schedule," she says, which I can tell from her less enthusiastic voice is a no. She glances at her watch and then looks down the block. "But, anyways, I've got a meeting with my agent that I really need to hurry to. It was great seeing you guys. I'll call you sometime!" The two Cindys make phone gestures with their hands and then are off down the street with their goodies.

"She seems to be handling this whole doubling thing quite well," Ahmed says with a sigh. "You know what? I think I'll take you up on that offer of hanging out at your place, if it's still open."

"It sure is. Let's finish these up and then hit up a dispensary on the way— I'm a bit dry on bud right now."

Thirty minutes later and we are in my apartment, sitting on a couch I had found on Craigslist in front of a TV also found on Craigslist. We take smoke breaks between bouts of tapping wildly at Xbox controllers and cursing at the screen. Ahmed leaves a few hours later with a smile on his face, and I spend the rest of the evening

41

trying to rid my mind from the day's earlier events.

I wake the next morning twisted in my sheets, an ache weighing me down, a stretching worry on my mind. I open my eyes and everything is wrong.

My vision has widened, and I'm pretty sure I have two noses. I look down at my bare body and witness—to my horror—my bellybutton has almost split into two separate ones (I dare not look down any farther). I'm not out of shape, but I don't work out much so it takes some effort to heave my body and extra weight up from the bed. The mirror calls me, and I stumble to the bathroom.

It takes a moment, maybe because I don't want the stretched face to be true, but the cause of my abnormal vision is what I feared most.

Queasiness takes over and I catch myself on the sink as the bathroom starts to spin. I try to spit into the drain, but my lips and mouth act strange and I only manage to dribble down my chin. I wipe away the spittle with my forearm, close my eyes, and take deep, slow breaths.

I do this until my heart steadies and then I reopen my eyes, wishing it only a nightmare, hallucinations left over from the dream-world.

It was not.

My body has become an imprint on Silly Putty, an unknown force in the universe acting like a child and pulling on both sides to create some humorous image. Everything is splitting right down the middle. If I take a moment, I can actually feel it happening.

Panic washes over me like a teenager waking up to discover the biggest nose pimple on school picture day. There is no way I am going out in public looking like the subject of an abstract painting, even if I could function properly—or need the money.

I get on the phone with my boss at Vidz Inc., a small video production company where I intern, and explain my situation.

"Ah, okay," he says. "Say no more. You can have the rest of the week off."

"Thanks, Mr. Hoffman," I say through slurred speech.

"Of course!" the bubbly man says. "My own transition was a doozy. Remember when I took that week off last month?" He answers for me. "I never told anyone because I didn't want to make a big deal out of it. When it was all over, I donated the extra body for a nice price. I'll give you the name of the company if you want."

"Uh, maybe."

"Oh, you're not planning on keeping it, are you? Boy, I do not recommend that. I'm sure you'll learn soon enough what a pain it is trying to control two bodies. It's not like you can just switch one of them off. Let me know next week what you decided. Or maybe I'll just see for myself, huh?" The other end chuckles. "You get some rest, though. You'll need it." He leaves it at that and hangs up.

I shoot Ahmed a text.

Me: It's happening to me.

He responds within minutes.

Ahmed: Whoa! You mean you're splitting?

Me: Yes.

Ahmed: You need me to come over?

Me: No. I think I'll be fine.

Ahmed: Okay. You let me know, though. It's a bit rough, so don't hesitate to call.

I wonder what to do with my day. I try to eat something, but my mouth doesn't want to function correctly. I try to drink something, but it feels weird swallowing into an expanding throat and stomach. Everything I do is impeded by my predicament. Even breathing is a little difficult—I can't imagine what my lungs are going through. I end up forcing down a painkiller leftover from a tooth extraction earlier in the year, needing it to take away the stretching I can feel upon my body, to numb my worrying.

By the evening, I have three eyes.

The process doesn't hurt, not in the classical sense of pain. It's more of an annoying strain on whatever part is replicating. The body seems to adapt to the situation, allowing for bodily functions so the person(s) can continue to live.

Cindy calls during the second day. She phones me up not long after my mouths have split, so it's a bit easier to talk and I answer.

"Ahmed told me the news," she opens with, only one of her.

Thanks, Ahmed.

"Yep," I say. "I've got the whole week off from work, but it shouldn't last more than another day or two, I would assume."

"Where are you at? In the separation?"

"I have no idea. Halfway? My heads are close to splitting, I think."

"Oh! You have to let me come over. I want to take a few pictures."

"What? No way! I don't want pictures of me like this. I look like a freak!"

"Don't say that. You're going through a natural thing."

"There is nothing natural about this."

"Oh, hush. I'm coming over."

"Cindy, no," I say, but the call has already ended.

The intercom to my apartment buzzes thirty minutes later. I pay no attention, but Cindy is stubborn and keeps her finger on the button for a good minute or two before I get irritated and reluctantly let her in. I open the door to the two of her.

"I'm so excited for you!" Both of them push past me and enter my studio. One plops on the couch and becomes distant while the other stays standing and gives me her full attention. "Take off those hats and blankets. There's no need to shy away from what I've already seen and gone through."

I take off the hats, but I leave the blanket tied around my abdomen because no clothes fit and I'd rather not wave around my pair of genitals in front of my friend.

Her face brightens as she gets a good look at me, and she says, "Cool, isn't it?"

"That's not the word I'd use," I say.

"Which is exactly the reason I wanted to talk to you." She sits on the couch and pats the empty seat in the middle.

I hesitate, but it's somewhat difficult to stand in my position. I sit with my back to the extra Cindy.

She jumps right into it. "I think you should keep your double."

"I doubt it."

"Oh, come on. Have you even thought about it?"

"Of course I have. It's *all* I've thought about. I can't wait for this ordeal to be over and done with. Plus, I could use the money I'll get from the research."

"Hey, it's not like I've been low on cash lately." She sighs and relaxes back into the couch. "But, yes, it can be an ordeal—you wouldn't believe how often I get distracted and trip. Sometimes I just want to strangle the other me, but I could never do that."

"Because of your career."

"No. Well, yes, but that's not the only reason. Scientists say we're connected through quantum entanglement, whatever that is, but it's more than that. She's a part of me. If she were gone, I'd feel as if something was missing from my core being. Honestly, I'm not even sure which one is the real me." Her index finger waved back and forth between my two bodies. "Do you know which one is your original self?"

I don't know what to say, sitting in silence as I mull over her words. Of course I know which one is the real me, don't I? She has sincerity in her eyes, and I can tell she truly believes what she said. My mind tilts but is not swayed.

"I'll think about it some more," I say.

"Good, that's all I ask for."

Her twin comes alive and then they both leave after giving me a pair of hugs. I think about calling Ahmed and cursing him out for telling Cindy, but I know he'd insist on coming over, too. Instead, as my body continues dividing, my friend's words run marathons around in my head.

I finish off my painkillers, smoke the rest of my pot, and patiently wait for the hideousness to end.

On the third day, my left and right wrists are the only body parts still connected. I count the seconds pass. My nerves itch for freedom. Finally, it happens.

My fingertips release as I am cleaning off one of my selves after a mishap involving the toilet and having to control two bowels at the same time. One of me is sitting on the ledge of the bathtub, and the other me is scrubbing away as hot water streams down my dirty legs. Curse words fly from my mouth. Annoyance has replaced disgust and shame. I wish for my normal life to return, and then the universe delivers.

The standing me, the aware me, is too shocked to register the separation, and the sitting me pitches forward without the connection and faceplants onto the tile floor. I swear I feel the pain in both of my heads. I leave my double—I think it's my double—sprawled out like a naked, drunken college student and jump around my small apartment with the joy of freedom.

I need to tell someone. I find my phone and call Ahmed.

"I'm free!"

Ahmed laughs. "Glad to hear it, man. It was quite something, huh?"

"It sure was. I'm just happy it's over and done with."

"Wait, did you already get rid of your double?"

I realize at this moment I'm having difficulty breathing. Well, one of me is. "I'll call you back," I say and hang up.

My mind switches bodies, and suddenly I find myself in the bathroom. My nose and mouth are scrunched against the floor in a way that blocks all airways. I lift myself, forgetting about my second body in the other room, and I hear a crash before feeling pain along my right side.

It's hard controlling two bodies at once.

I focus, splitting my thoughts and actions between two physical perspectives. Half of me is in the bathroom, and the other half is strewn about a broken coffee table, a flipped ashtray, and the stinky remains of a shattered bong. I stand, brush off some debris, and convene on the couch.

I've already lost track of which is the real me. Truth be told, I don't think I ever knew. We look exactly the same, right down to the three moles in the shape of a triangle above my right hip. The circumcision translated as well. I raise my right hands, expecting a mirror image, but of course that doesn't happen—stupid.

This creates a dilemma, and it's not the only one.

Cindy was right. I feel a connection between the two of us. Whether it be quantum entanglement or something deeper, both bodies feel like my own.

My mind is torn.

There's only one question on my mind.

"So, what did you do with yourself?"

Ahmed's leg bounces up and down. We're sitting at the bar attached to Suckle This Chuckle, a comedy club where Ahmed works as manager and often performs. Both of us have a beer in our hands, but the sweet taste of bourbon tickles my tongue as if from another universe—another me. I haven't said a word to my friend since the other day, and I know he's itching for the end result.

"I decided to keep my double," I say with a knowing grin. "I found a business that will double the amount most government agencies hand out, but that's over the course of a few years. I get a monthly check until I say when."

Ahmed whistles. "That has to be a lot. The government is trying to get their grubby hands on as many dou-bles as possible." He raises an eyebrow. "You didn't..."

My smile widens, and the arousal of a phantom wet dream stirs in my pants. I push the sensation behind an afterthought, keeping with my current self.

Laughing so hard beer dribbles from his mouth: "You are such a dirty whore!"

I shrug. "Isn't that what everyone uses their double for, whoring them out for money in one way or another? Besides, I only agreed if there were certain rules set in place—I'm not a complete degenerate. I can quit whenever, but they keep me pampered and paid."

"Madame Horowitz's Company of Pleasure?"

I nod. The business specializes in those who enjoy pleasure and can afford a bit more. Doubles are a unique kink among certain people, even when only one of the doubles is involved—I don't judge.

Ahmed is shaking his head, the remnants of laughter heaving his chest. "I thought about going down that route, but I couldn't handle controlling another body. I think I'd spend too much time in the one having fun."

"I slip in every now and then," I say with no shame. For the briefest of seconds, gentle fingers grip my sides in mutual ecstasy. I shake it off, finding it more and more difficult to keep with my present body. "You're off now, right? I bribed the Cindys into a quick latte date in exchange for gossip on my double."

"Gossip: the one bait that can lure the Cindys into hanging out. Sure, I'm in. She'll have a fit once you tell her where your other half is."

I roll my eyes. As if the Cindys were a pair of Mother Theresas. "Whatever. Like she didn't do the same thing when she first split."

"No! Did she? She didn't. Really? She never told me that."

"Watch her face when I explain my situation. Her reaction will give away the truth."

We down our beers and leave. Instead of putting it on his tab, I insist on paying for us both. It's nice and comforting knowing money is no longer a worry. We cut through a park on our way, lighting a joint between us to prepare for our meeting.

The Quantum Twinsies can be a handful at times.

About the Author

Michael Shimek current lives in Colorado where he writes and has adventures in the mountains. He has stories that appear in Sanitarium Magazine Issue #32, *Fossil Lake: An Anthology of the Aberrant, Fossil Lake III: Unicornado!, We Walk Invisible, In Shambles: A Scarlet Nightmare Vol. II, Slaughter House: The Serial Killer Edition-Vol. I, A Chemerical World: Tales of the Unseelie Court*, and more. Many of his stories can be found for free on his website: ww.michaelshimeck.blogspot.com. He also tweets @michaelshimek.

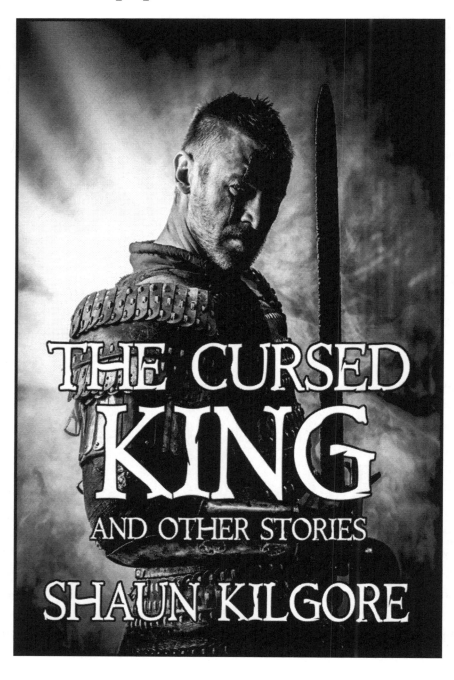

THE DOOR

BY JON GAUTHIER

When Collins first saw the door, he didn't even notice it. He was in his usual morning stupor and on his way to the kitchen, the haze of sleep still muddying both his vision and his mind. Curious things, no matter how curious, seem to go unnoticed before the brain is completely awake. So, Collins walked right past the door, completely oblivious to it. He busied himself in the kitchen for a while, drinking coffee and making eggs and toast.

After washing the dishes and pouring another mug of coffee, Collins stepped out of the kitchen and into the hallway, fully intent on going up to his office to begin grading papers. He saw the door again—really saw it. It was centred between the two antique pedestal tables, taking up a section of wall where a painting of the Canadian Rockies was supposed to hang. It was a little over six feet high and two-and-a-half feet wide, made of dark oak planks and decorated with a few dozen rivets that had been arranged into eight simple squares. About halfway up its right side was an ancient looking copper knob with a small keyhole.

Collins stared at the door for a full minute. He knew it shouldn't be there. He knew it had certainly not been there the night before. Or the night before that. Or the night before that. In fact, having lived in this house for his entire life, Collins knew that this particular door had never existed— not even before the renovation his father had done in the early 90s. The door, quite simply, wasn't supposed to exist.

"Well, that's not right," Collins said to himself. It was the first and only thing he could think to say. He looked into his coffee mug, expecting to see a hallucinogenic substance floating around—something that would explain this phenomenon. Then he took a sip of the coffee, hoping another blast of caffeine would solve the problem. The door, of course, stayed in where it was. Collins set the mug down on one of the pedestal tables where it instantly looked out-of-place next to the 16th Century sextant and marine compass. Then he reached his hand out towards the door.

He hesitated. "Touching it will make it real," Collins said in a warning tone. "If you go upstairs and forget about it, it will disappear." He ignored himself and pressed the tips of his fingers to the dark wood. He was both surprised and disappointed at how perfectly normal it felt. He ran his hand along the oak, which had a slightly rough texture. The metal rivets were cold and smooth. He tried to give one a gentle twist, just to see if it would come off. It didn't. Finally, he took in a breath and wrapped his hand around the doorknob. Since the door was on an exterior wall, Collins knew that it couldn't possibly lead anywhere but to the back yard. There was absolutely no chance of it leading to some kind of dungeon or sacrificial chamber.

Or was there?

Collins let go of the doorknob.

If the door had appeared overnight, maybe another room had as well. Maybe a complete wing had been added to the house. Collins backed away. He went into the kitchen and opened the back door. Sticking his head out into the chilly December morning, Collins looked at the rear of the house. There was no other room; no newly-added wing; nothing for the door to lead into. What was stranger, though, was the other side of the door wasn't there. In the spot where the door should have stood was the same section of brick wall that had been there since the house was built. The door, it seemed, led nowhere.

"Now, how do you explain that?" Collins inquired to no one.

The door was still there when he returned to the hallway. He grabbed the doorknob, twisted, and pulled. Nothing happened. The door didn't budge. He tried pushing, and still nothing. There wasn't even the slightest hint of movement. Collins let out a soft chuckle and let go of the knob.

"Locked. Of course."

It was mid-afternoon, and Collins was sitting in his office. On his desk, an uneaten sandwich lay next to a stack of still ungraded papers. He was staring out window and into the street. Juniper Crescent was a fairly small and uninteresting bit of street that sat nearly forgotten in the southwest corner of the city. From his office chair, Collins could see into his neighbours' living room window. Their Christmas tree was now up and decorated, a colourful pile of gifts already congealed at its base. Collins found the notion of Christmas trees to be equal parts irritating and bizarre. As a professor of Gothic English Literature, Collins usually had a soft spot for the bizarre for the uncanny. Christmas trees, though…

"It was locked," Collins suddenly said, snapping himself out of his grumpy considerations. "Why would it be locked? And where is the key?" They were good questions. There was a keyhole, which meant that there had to be a key. Did the key appear with the door? And, if so, where was it? Collins pushed away from his desk, left the office, and headed down the stairs, his bathrobe fluttering behind him like a cape.

"And if the key didn't appear, then why not," he asked. "What good is a locked door with no key?"

Collins walked into the hallway. The door was still standing between the two pedestal tables.

"Your key," Collins said to it. "Where is your key?" He approached the left table and looked behind the sextant and compass. He then lifted each piece up to look under them. He looked at their bottoms, thinking maybe the key had been taped to one of them.

"But who would have taped it?" he wondered aloud.

With the left table thoroughly searched, he moved on to the right one, which held an assortment of horse figurines—the finer pieces from his late mother's collection (the rest of which was boxed away in the attic). Collins picked up each figurine and shook it, thinking maybe the key was hidden inside. When the final figure was set back down, Collins dropped to his knees and looked under the table. Nothing. He crawled over to the left table and looked under it. Nothing. Collins let out a huff and got back to his feet.

"Where?" he asked. "Where did they put it?" He didn't know who 'they' were, and knew that was the more important question, but he didn't have the courage to ask it aloud.

Collins went into the living room. He searched all the possible places the key could be hidden. The bookshelves, the television stand, the assortment of maple and hickory chests his grandfather had built, and the dozens of other nooks and crannies that can be found in old rooms. Collins approached the sofa and flung off the cushions. As he looked in the crevices, he thought of all the other rooms that would have to be searched. The key could anywhere.

"The kitchen," he muttered as he dug through the bowels of the sofa. "The powder room; the laundry room; the dining room; the bedrooms; the bathroom; the attic; the basement— Oh, God, the basement." The basement would take days to search. A house was a massive place when you were searching for something—especially something you weren't even sure existed.

"It has to exist," Collins said. "How could it even have been locked without a key?"

"What if it was locked from the other side?"

"There is no other side!"

"Of course there if," he calmly replied. "Nothing has only one side."

Collins stopped, a thin layer of ice crawling up his body. "Calm down," he said. "Calm down and keep searching." He obeyed and moved on to the bookshelf.

He was sitting on the basement staircase, his feet on the bottom step and his face in his hands. His eyes were dry and puffy, and his neck was red with a rash—the result of rummaging around in 50 years' worth of dust and cobwebs. Two days had passed since he'd discovered the door. Two days spent searching the entire house for the key. Two days with little-to-no food or sleep. Somewhere in the back of his mind, he knew he was supposed to be at the University. But that didn't matter. The only thing that concerned him was opening the door.

He'd searched the entire house. Everywhere. Every room. Every closet. Every box. Every cupboard. Every dish. Every closet. He'd moved every piece of furniture, and shaken out every book. He had searched every single inch of the house that was pos-sible to search, and they key was no-where to be found. He had, though, found a few lost items that had long since been forgotten about: an old record needle had been wedged be-tween the carpet and baseboard in the corner of the living room; the ear-ring of his third (and last) long-term partner, Vanessa, had been hiding in the box spring of his bed; and his fa-ther's favorite cigarette lighter had been resting on top of an air duct in the basement ceiling, undoubtedly having been used as a makeshift flash-light during one of the many times his father examined the pipes.

Collins pulled the lighter out of his pocket and sparked it to life. He stared into the quaking flame, won-dering what to do next. "We'll have to rip out the carpets," he whispered. "Then the floorboards. Then we start looking in the walls. After that, we start pulling up shingles. Then we dig up the yard."

Collins got back to his feet, stuffing the lighter into the pocket of his housecoat, and started to make his way back up the stairs. As he reached to switch off the basement lights, he noticed the row of tools that hung on the wall just inside the basement door. They were items that one may need quick access to during the nor-mal course of home ownership: as-sorted screwdrivers, an adjustable wrench, a tape measure, a boxcutter, and a hammer. Collins stared at the implements, a new idea forming in his exhausted mind. He grabbed the screwdrivers and the hammer and stepped up into the hallway.

Barely noticing what he was doing, Collins approached one of the pedestal tables and knocked all the horse figurines off with a swipe of his arm. The equines fell unceremoniously to the floor and shattered into a white stain of ceramic splinters. He set the tools on the table and then went to the coat closet where he retrieved his recently-dry cleaned blazer. He pulled out the wire hanger and let the plastic-covered garment fall to the floor. Untwisting and straightening the hanger, Collins then made his way into the garage. The frozen concrete floor burned his feet as he hurried to the worktable and grabbed a pair of wire cutters. With a few quick snips, Collins had three six-inch pieces of hanger. He grabbed the splitting axe and sledge out of the corner and went back inside.

Just as stepped back into the house, the doorbell rang. Collins' heart leapt and his grip softened. The two heavy tools fell from his hands and clunked noisily on the hardwood.

"Professor Collins?" a voice called from the other side of the door. It was Jonas Mallory, Collins' teacher's assistant.

Collins went perfectly still. "Stay quiet," he whispered. "Just stay quiet and he won't know you're here." A part of him—the part that was still connected to the normal world—felt guilty. Collins had been AWOL for two days now. He'd missed his office hours, and hadn't replied to any emails or phone calls. It was perfectly reasonable for Jonas to be worried about him. He was Collins' only real friend. So, that still sane sliver of his mind desperately wanted to open the door and assure Jonas that everything was okay and that he would be back in the office in a couple of days.

The doorknob jiggled. "Professor, I'm coming inside. Okay?" The door began to open and Collins instantly rushed to it, slamming it back against Jonas, who cried out in surprise.

"Jesus! Professor Collins, is that you?"

"I'm fine," Collins answered. He said it too quickly. Too bizarrely. He instantly recognized that he most definitely did not sound fine.

"What's going on?" Jonas sounded even more concerned now. "I've been trying to get a hol..."

"I've been ill," Collins said, interrupting him. "A really nasty bug, I'm afraid. I've barely been able to get out of bed." As he spoke, he slid his hand up and twisted the deadbolt into place.

"Well, you could have at least emailed or texted me," Jonas said. His concern was slowly morphing into annoyance. "The third-year students expected their papers back yesterday. And the exams..."

"You can grade the papers," Collins blurted out. Or was it the other Collins? It was difficult to tell now.

"But, you've never let..." Jonas fumbled over his words. "Wait a minute," he continued, his tone suggesting that he'd come a realization. "You mean you haven't even graded them yet?"

"A few," Collins said. This was the truth.

Jonas didn't reply for a couple of seconds. Finally he let out a sigh and said, "Okay. That's fine. I guess."

With that, Collins rushed up the stairs and into his office. Unlike some of the other rooms, which had been turned into complete shambles during the search for the key, the office was still perfectly tidy. Collins had searched it after the living room, and, at that point, still had enough sense to not just toss things around. The papers were stacked neatly on the desk. Collins grabbed the pile and made his way back downstairs.

"Ok, Jonas," Collins said as he approached the front door again. "I'm going to slide them through." He undid the lock, turned the knob, and slid the door open just wide enough to slip the papers through. As he did, he caught Jonas' eyes, which widened at the sight of him.

"Jesus, Professor. You look like Hell." Jonas sounded genuinely concerned—shocked, even. Collins handed off the papers and quickly closed the door, hoping that Jonas would take the hint and leave him alone.

"I... I'll check in on you tomorrow," Jonas muttered, his voice flat and somewhat defeated.

"Ok, then," Collins said. "Thank you, Jonas."

There was no answer after that.

Collins sat on the floor, leaning against the door. His arms, shoulders and back ached and he was coated in a slick layer of sweat. He was breathing heavily, and could even feel tears starting to well up in his swollen eyes.

"What are you?" He whispered. "What are you, and where did you come from?"

The pieces of hanger hadn't worked. He'd realized very quickly that he didn't even know how to pick a lock. The small tools hadn't worked either. He'd tried to pry the door open by hammering the screwdriver into the space between the door and the frame, but the screwdriver wouldn't go it. It hadn't even dug any of the wood out, which is what he'd really expected to happen. He'd finally tried hammering the screwdriver into the keyhole, in the hopes of breaking whatever ancient mechanism was inside, but that hadn't worked either.

After exhausting all the options with the small tools, Collins had pulled out the heavy artillery. The sledge had been first. He'd struck it against the door knob at least two-dozen times and it bounced off every single time, not even denting or scuffing the copper. The axe had been next. He'd heaved its head into dark oak one... twice... three times... and nothing happened. The axe had bounced off the wood as if it were made of rubber. The flat and lifeless sound it had made was something Collins had never heard before. It was as if the door was dead and led to a dead place. The axe had done nothing to the wood. Not even the slightest chip had appeared.

Collins forced himself to his feet, fighting every urge within him just to lie down and fall into a deep and unending sleep. He grabbed the sledge and made his way to the kitchen. "I'll try from the other side," he said. "Maybe it will open from the other side."

Collins slipped into his boots and went out the back door. The afternoon was bright and cold and a fresh layer of snow covered the yard. Collins approached the back wall and, without hesitation, slammed the

sledge into it. The brick, which was old and brittle, started to break away after a few swings. Collins dropped the sledge and pulled the loose bricks away. Behind them was a layer of wood panelling that had been cracked by the sledge. Collins dug his fingers into the crack and tugged on the panelling, tearing it apart like paper. At a time when the door didn't exist, that would have revealed the wall studs and insulation, but, instead, it revealed a dark slab of oak augmented with small metal rivets.

"There you are," Collins whispered. He grabbed the sledge and bashed at the wall a dozen more times, stopping only to tear away the brick and the wood panelling. Finally, with his heart racing and sweat freezing on his skin, Collins pulled off the last piece of wood and stepped back.

The back of the door (or was it the front?) was now fully exposed by the jagged hole that he'd torn in the back of his house. Collins grabbed the doorknob and tried to turn it. Nothing happened. Rage thundered through him.

Collins screamed, "Please, just tell me what I have to do. How do I open it?"

"It can't be opened," he answered. It was in that voice again—the voice that was impossibly calm and wasn't his. "Not from this world."

Collins let out a furious cry and grabbed the sledge. He smashed it against the door with an incredible burst of strength. Again and again he slammed the steel head of the sledge into the door, and again and again it hit the wood with that pathetic, rubbery thump. When he could no long hold the sledge, Collins collapsed into the pile of rubble at his feet and fell against the door, pounding it with his fists like a child who had been sent to his room.

Sobbing freely, he pressed the side of his face against the door. He then noticed, somewhere in the chaos, that the door was warm. It was far too warm considering how cold it was outside. Collins went silent, but continued to take large heaving breaths. He rubbed his eyes and nose on the sleeve of his housecoat and slowly recomposed himself.

"How can it be warm?" he asked.

"Because it's not actually here," he answered. "Don't you understand? It's somewhere else. You're seeing it by accident."

A defeated moan slid from Collins' mouth as he folded onto his knees. With the last bit of strength he could muster, Collins crawled back toward the house.

Jonas Mallory brought his beat-up Hyundai to a stop right behind Professor Collins' 20-year-old Subaru. He'd known Collins for four years, and in all that time he'd never known him to be as flaky as he'd been over the past few days. He'd never seen the man miss a single class or even take a sick day. He always returned assignments and exams promptly, and he never ignored emails or phone calls—not even when he was on vacation or when school was out of session.

Jonas put his car into park and stepped out of it. He ducked his face into the collar of his jacket and jogged up to Collins' front door. When Jonas had come to the house two days earlier, Collins was a mess. He'd looked like he'd aged two decades—like his very life was being consumed by some mysterious entity.

Jonas knocked.

"Professor Collins?" he shouted.

No response.

He knocked even harder.

"Professor Collins, are you ok?"

No response.

Jonas let out an irritated sigh, turned the doorknob and stepped into the house. The stench of gasoline slammed into him like a freight train.

"Profess..." The word evaporated before Jonas even finished uttering it. He froze.

Collins was in a heap on the floor, his back up against a door. Tools and broken glass were strewn all around him. He reminded Jonas of a dummy someone would put on their front porch on Halloween. He was wearing the same disheveled housecoat and pajamas he'd been wearing two days earlier. His face was deathly white, but streaked with red splotches that also dotted his neck. His eyes were sunken and encased in pitch-black circles—and wide open, staring up into an oblivion that was only visible to him. His arms lay at his side like two dead snakes.

Jonas moved towards him slowly, trying to process the sight of his mentor and best friend in such disarray. "Professor Collins," he said it softly, as if trying not to wake him up. As he got closer, he was suddenly struck by the smell of body odour. It mixed with the gasoline and hung there in a viscous cloud. Jonas knelt down and put a hand on Collins' ankle when, suddenly, the professor screamed and burst into alertness. Jonas jumped back.

"For Christ's sake!" he cried.

Collins was gasping for breath and starring wide-eyed at Jonas as if trying to decipher a new reality. Finally, his breathing steadied.

"Jonas," he murmured. "You're here."

"What the Hell happened to you?" Jonas demanded. "What's going on? Why does it smell like gas in here?"

Collins face was twitching. It looked like he was fighting back tears. "Do you have the key?" he asked.

Jonas ignored him and rose to his feet. "I'm going to call you an ambulance."

Collins let out a small psychotic laugh. It was more like a giggle—like he was a little boy who just told his first dirty joke. Then his face became very serious and he moved his gaze back towards the invisible oblivion.

"Do you think there are other places, Jonas?" His voice was laced with a hazy and manic exhaustion.

"Professor, just take it easy," Jonas said. He had his phone out now, and was dialing 9-1-1.

"Maybe the people from one of those places put it there."

The 9-1-1 operator answered and Jonas requested an ambulance to Collins' address. When he disconnected, he noticed that Collins had something in his hand—a lighter. Jonas stomach dropped as he realized Collins' intentions. The stench of gasoline seemed even stronger now.

Jonas dropped his phone. "Professor," he said softly. "Professor, give me that." He knelt down slowly, reaching for the lighter.

"It's the only way to open it," Collins said. He was almost unrecognisable now. He had the face and voice of a madman.

Jonas lunged at him, grabbing for the lighter as he did. Collins let out a scream and tried to twist away, but Jonas, who was far bigger, younger, and not under a maniacal spell, was able to pin him down and wrestle the lighter from his frail grasp.

"No!" Collins screamed. He sounded as if he'd been yanked onto another level of coherence. "We have to let them in!"

Jonas got back to his feet, bent down and swept Collins up from the floor. At six feet, two inches, this was a relatively easy task for him. Collins was short, and couldn't have weighed more than 150 pounds. Jonas threw Collins over his shoulder, not even realizing how incredibly bizarre such an act was. In the classroom, Collins was an imposing and intimidating figure to Jonas—an academic Leviathan—but, in that moment, he was nothing more than a sick old man that had to be rescued.

Jonas turned and trudged to the front door. As he stepped out into the chilly evening air, Jonas set Collins down on the porch. The professor was unconscious now—passed out from exhaustion.

"It'll be okay, professor," Jonas said as he removed his coat and laid it over Collins. "We'll get you some help."

He brushed snow off a deck chair and sat down, trying his best to relax and recalibrate his mind. The sound of approaching sires grew louder and louder, shattering the quiet and picture-perfect illusion of the neighbourhood.

Somewhere else, Joanna Mallory brought her beat-up Hyundai to a stop right behind Instructor Collins' 20-year-old Okami. She'd known Collins for four years, and in all that time, she'd never known him to be as flaky as he'd been over the past few days. She'd never seen the man miss a single class or even take a sick day. He always returned assignments and exams promptly, and he never ignored emails or phone calls—not even when he was on vacation or when school was out of session.

Joanna put her car into park and stepped out of it. She ducked her face into the collar of her jacket and jogged up to Collins' front door. When Joanna had come to the house two days earlier, Collins was a mess. He'd looked like he'd aged two decades—like his very life was being consumed by some mysterious entity.

Joanna knocked.

"Instructor Collins?" she shouted.

No response.

She knocked harder. "Instructor Collins, are you ok?"

No response.

Joanna let out an irritated sigh, turned the doorknob and stepped into the house. Her eyes were immediately drawn to the opposite wall where Collin's lay in a heap. He was wearing the same ratty room-jacket and pyjamas that he'd been wearing two days earlier. His skin had taken on a slight shade of yellow and his eyes were glazed over and fixed on the ceiling. For a moment, Joanna feared he was dead.

"Instructor Collins?" She spoke with a quiet apprehension, as if she was afraid he was going to spring to life and attack her. She moved towards him, remaining focused on his wide vitric gaze.

"Instructor, are you all right?" When she reached him, she knelt down and touched his cheek with the back of her hand. His skin was warm. He wasn't dead.

"Instructor!"

He blinked four times in rapid succession. His eyes darted about the room and stopped when they met hers. Lucidity returned to his face.

"Joanna," he said. His voice was hoarse.

She put a hand on his shoulder. "Instructor, what happ…"

"It's gone," he said, interrupting her. "The door is gone."

Joanna felt her brow furrow. "What are you…"

"The door! The door to the wine cellar," he cried. "Look!"

He cast a finger to the wall behind them and Joanna turned her head. For the first time since stepping into the house, she saw it. The door that led to Instructor Collins' wine cellar was indeed gone. Joanna was surprised that she hadn't noticed it earlier. She'd been in Collins' house a few times before, and the door to the wine cellar was always incredibly prominent, standing between the two pedestal tables that held his collection of model ships. In place of the door, the wall that had once surrounded it was now complete, and hanging on it was a framed painting of a mountain landscape. Joanna blinked at the foreign sight and turned her gaze to Collins.

"You've walled it up," she said. It came out as a question.

Collins shook his head. "No. I just came downstairs and it was like this."

Joann furrowed her brow and massaged her temple. "Instructor, I've been grading papers for the past two days—not to mention trying to keep Doctor Bryson from discovering you've been missing in action since…"

"Don't you get it, Joanna," Collins said, interrupting her. "It's *gone*."

Joanna looked up again at the wall where the door had once been.

"How were you able to match the wallpaper?" she asked. "That stuff must be fifty years old."

Collins shook his head and his face suddenly took on a vacant, almost dreamy look. "The wallpaper's not from here," he said quietly. "It's from wherever the door went. The painting, too."

Joanna let out another sigh and got to her feet. "Instructor, I don't know what this is all about, but I think I need to take you to the hospital. You're obviously not well."

"Look in the backyard," Collins said.

"Instructor, I..."

"Just look!" he screamed. His face had suddenly gone red, and his eyes were wide. Joanna flinched and felt a wave of shock go through her. She'd never seen Collins so animated, let alone angry. She decided to placate him for only a few more minutes before calling the paramedics, and walked into the kitchen.

When she opened the back door, her stomach dropped. The narrow outcropping of exterior wall that surrounded the wine cellar stairwell had been completely destroyed. The yard was littered with a mess of crushed bricks and shredded wood and insulation, and a variety of tools. Joanna stepped into the yard and made her way across the rubble to the stairwell. Looking down into the darkness, she saw that the old stone stairs were covered in snow. She then looked at the wall that the stairwell jutted from.

The bricks, wood and insulation, had been torn away, leaving nothing but the back of the interior panelling.

"Instructor," Joanna said with a sigh. "What the Hell have you been doing?" She pressed her palm to the panelling and was surprised by how warm it was despite the chill in the air. Joanna made a fist and rapped her knuckles against the wood. The sound was not like anything she'd ever heard before—and it certainly was not what knuckles on wood should sound like. The sound was dull and muted—like it wasn't actually occurring. Joanna felt a chill pass through her and she rushed back into the house.

"I tried smashing right through," Collins said as soon as she returned to the hallway. He was standing up now, facing the wall where the door had been. "From both sides. I used a sledge, an axe... nothing worked."

"It's not possible," Joanna mumbled.

"I thought the wine cellar would be gone too," Collins said. "But it's still there. Only the door is gone. It's like it was..."

"Swapped," Joanna said. Collin's turned towards her, a relieved smile growing on his face.

"Exactly," he said.

"But, how?" Joanna asked.

"A glitch," Collins said quietly. "I think it was some kind of glitch in... in the way things are."

Joanna gave an idle nod, her eyes unable to leave the painting of the mountain landscape.

"The bigger question, though," Collins continued, "is 'can it still be opened?'"

Joanna looked at him. "Can it?"

"I think so."

"How?"

Collins patted the side of his right thigh and said "Because the key's gone too."

"It could be any number things," the doctor said quietly. Jonas listened but didn't take his eyes off the hospital bed where Professor Collins lay unconscious, tubes and wires snaking out of him and into a variety of machines.

"Did he have any mental health issues?" the doctor asked. "Anything in his family history?"

Jonas shook his head. "Not that I know of."

"Well, he's going to be admitted to the psychiatric ward. After he wakes up, of course."

"He's not crazy," Jonas said, his voice taking on a defensive edge.

"I'm not saying he is, but to do something like he did—to almost set himself and his home on fire... it's very troubling behavior. We have to run some analysis."

Jonas gave a glum, conceding nod. "I guess that makes sense."

The doctor put and hand on Jonas' shoulder and began to guide him out of the hospital room. "We'll need you to sign some forms," he said. "You're listed as his next of kin."

The doctor left him at the nurse's station, where Jonas was handed a small stack of papers. He began scanning the documents and signing his name where required and was about halfway through when the nurse said "Oh, there was one other thing." She set something on the desk next to the papers, a small *clack* sounding when the object made contact with the wood. Jonas looked over to see that it was a small copper key.

Professor Collins' words immediately echoed in his mind: *Do you have the key?*

"It was in one of the pockets of his pajama pants," the nurse said, responding to a question Jonas hadn't asked. Jonas picked the key up off the desk, muttered "Thanks," and slid it into his jacket pocket. The nurse gave a quick nod and Jonas turned his focus back to the forms, the weight of the key tugging at him like a living thing.

Quiet was all he knew. Quiet, cement, steel, cold, and doctors.

61

Sometimes he thought. He'd once been someone important. The memories floated there like soap bubbles, transparent and fragile—wet representations of reality dancing away in his broken mind, always out of grasp.

He lay still, the medication going to work, pulling a dark curtain up over his toes, his feet, his ankles…crawling up his body like a grey winter chill. Collins knew sleep would soon follow. Then, somewhere in the pitch-black hypnagogia that enveloped him, he heard the unmistakable sound of a door opening.

About the Author

Jon Gauthier is a horror and science-fiction writer who fell in love with both genres after discovering *Jurassic Park, Goosebumps,* and *Scary Stories to Tell in the Dark* when he was 8 years old. His work has been published by DarkFuse and Digital Fiction Publishing. Jon currently lives in Ottawa, Ontario with his wife and daughter, and dozens of uncooperative partially-finished stories.

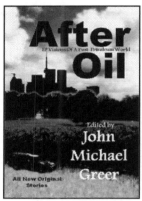

RECYCLED

BY MAREE BRITTENFORD

I think I understand why people kill themselves by jumping off bridges.

The urge to stand at the edge and look down is irresistible for the average person. For a mind in a certain state the temptation to take one more step must be strong.

Not that anyone could jump off this bridge. The long tube is fully enclosed, made of a flexible acrylic material. The transition between the two stations made easy and safe.

Calling it a bridge feels like a lie. I remember bridges. The real kind where wind blows and you can smell mud and plants and water. Not the sterile blend of recycled air that they pump through this place. It smells like wildflowers today, or a chemical approximation of it. The scent sticks to my throat with its falseness. It covers the smell of unwashed bodies, perhaps it's how the Managers pretend that they're treating us humanely. They are. We have the same level of human rights as prisoners, three minute showers every four days.

I still can't resist lingering on the bridge, as people have done for thousands of years, only instead of staring into flowing water I'm staring down at the planet floating in the blackness. I've never been there, none of us have. I wonder what they think of us, if they think of us at all. Perhaps none of them ever look up and notice the star that moves oddly across the sky, or spare a thought for the thousands of people locked into an endless orbit around their planet.

I rest my head against the viewing window, resenting them for their happy ignorance. The acrylic should be cold, but the properties of the material prevent transfer of the external temperatures, so it's the same temperature as the interior environment, meeting the legally mandated 15 degrees Celsius.

Will the refugees here ever stand on a real bridge again, or are they bound to be trapped in this perfectly controlled environment for the rest of an unnatural life?

I feel a hand brush across my shoulder, and flinch instinctively. "Rana, you'll be late."

It's only Shen, and I let my fists relax. In this cramped bubble we guard our personal space vigilantly. Especially me, a girl alone. I don't know where my parents are, I assume they're dead. I was smuggled off-world with a group of other children, hidden amongst bolts of fabric, almost suffocated by the heavy cloth before I was discovered and sent to a Refuge. They told me they'd be coming for me soon. That was ten years ago.

Ten years that I've been in orbit. They call them Refuges. Old stations and passenger ships, cobbled together into long term housing. This is one of a dozen that orbit the planets in this system, reluctantly maintained with money from a patchwork of treaties and charities in this sector.

We've been circling her for ten long years while they try to decide what to do with us, an entire planet's worth of Refugees, citizens of no-where, that no one wants. So we circle, locked in orbit while our lives are locked in bureaucracy run by faceless people on the planets below.

I am going to be late, so I hurry to my work assignment, at the refinery, sorting scrap metal supposedly bound for recycling. I don't know why I bother to go. Habit I suppose.

It's busy work, designed to keep us exhausted and mindless. And it works for the most part. It took me years to figure out that we were sorting the same junk repeatedly. I think I'm one of the few who knows.

I only noticed because of my side business. I was lucky I suppose, that when I got thrown into the population I was taken in by an old woman who didn't treat me too bad. She didn't care much for me either, but it wasn't harsh. And she taught me things, made me a sort of an apprentice. I learned to fix things, small things, the sort of things that people brought with them when they were rushed off-planet, small devices that could be slipped into pockets and carried along. Things that over the years have broken down, and been sold when things got tight. Not weapons, I won't touch those, although I know they're out there. It's not worth my neck to attract the attention of Management over it, when there's so many benign objects needing repairs.

Of course Management sees us fed, clothed, and housed, with access to medical care, as per the Radley Planetary Convention Agreement of Refugee Rights, but no more than that, and food comes in the form of ration packs dispensed at the end of each twelve-hour work shift. So if you miss, but aren't under medical care, then you go hungry.

That convention is the reason none of us have ever set foot on that planet, hanging so tauntingly beautiful, outside the windows. I don't know that for sure, but there's a rumor that if someone even sets one foot on the planet then they have to let you stay. In the early years apparently there was a lot of stowing away on the transfer ships that bring the Managers back and forth. I was very young then, but I remember them trying. As far as I know nobody ever succeeded, and it's been years since an attempt has been made. The monotony has ground us all down, I guess.

I take my place at the conveyor, seconds before the siren sounds and the junk starts tumbling down the chute. I prepare myself to do the absolute minimum, and keep my eyes open for useful parts.

The parts are how I figured out the sham. It was back when I'd first been put on this line, when I'd reached age twelve, according to earth years, the system of measurement enforced on us by the Managers. Apparently we'd gone shockingly native back on Relevo, counting our ages by the circuits our own planet made around its own star.

I've gotten used to the earth years. It's not as if I'll ever be going back.

Back when I started on the line things had been newer, and life still had a little optimism. I was younger and I'd only been a refugee for five years, so I still dreamed that my parents would arrive and take me home, or at the very least I'd be rehomed on a planet. The old woman and I had been fixing things by cannibalizing parts from other devices, but the resources were starting to run out. The same bits break down in everything, and we were getting desperate. She was too old to stand at the conveyor, and the small amount of food allotted to us wasn't enough to feed us both without the extra we bartered by the repairs.

Then, one day on the line, I'd seen a tangle of wire go by, spiderweb thin, and I'd wanted it. I was too slow, some other hands with longer reach had reached out and scooped it into a basket, and it was gone.

I'd mourned that tangle of wire, imagining all the things I could've done with it.

Until I saw it pass by again a few weeks later. I was faster that time, plunging the twisted bundle down inside my shirt where it scratched at me for the rest of my shift.

I'd taken it back to my bunk and hidden it inside a fold of blanket. The old woman discovered it almost immediately, crowing with delight. That wire lasted a long time, and kept us well. She demanded I steal more.

And I began to notice that even when I missed out on snatching up some valuable piece of scrap, it would come back around a week or two later. I started marking things, with little scratches, not quite willing to believe, but it all came back around. All of it.

It was when it sunk in: our work was pointless. We stood at a conveyor, two twelve-hour shifts each day, sorting scrap that was destined, not for recycling in the sense of being made into new items as we had all assumed, but was instead recycled only by going past us for sorting again and again.

Perhaps I should've told. Gotten angry. Stirred something up. But it broke that last shred of optimism in me. This was my life, my future. Cycling junk around a conveyor, never to be made into something new, cycling in space around a planet, never to be allowed to be made into a real person, with a home.

I kept cycling too, what else was there? Stealing from the belt didn't seem wrong. After all, what was I doing but actually reusing it? The Managers didn't care, they still don't. As long as I'm not making weapons, I'm making their lives easier. Keeping the population content with their little toys.

At the end of my shift I head back to my bunk space. I have it good. When I'd come back to find the old woman cold and still on the bunk below mine two years ago I'd expected the berth to be reassigned, but it didn't happen, so I've taken it over as my workshop. No one complains. They like the repairs more than they want to fight over a single bunk. I pull the curtain across the alcove, shutting myself into my own private space, another privilege my skills have earned me. Privacy.

Privacy is probably the highest commodity possible around here. I start to empty my haul out of my pockets when I hear a tap on the wall outside.

"Come in," I sigh, already knowing who it is. No one else knocks like that.

Shen pops his head around the corner and smiles. He's one of the few people left around here that can smile like that. He lives here like the rest of us, but somehow they can't quite break him down. He's the closest thing I have to a friend, although I wouldn't quite call him that. I don't have friends, really. Oh, I had them when I was young, back on Relevo, before it all went to hell, but when you see people die for no reason, and then find yourself shuffled into space and then dumped into a place like this, you learn how little people really care. And how to take care of yourself, by yourself, not to rely too much on anyone.

Shen slips between the curtain and the wall, barely stirring it with his passage, and slides down onto the bunk. "You get a good haul?" he asks. I shrug and finish emptying out my take. It's not much. I didn't have my head in it. He empties his own pockets too, depositing his own measly gatherings. He always claims it's because his own spot on the line is further down from me, so I get the good stuff first. It's really that he just doesn't have much of an eye for it.

I open up the panel in the wall and carefully stow away the parts. I hesitate for a moment, and then put it back in place without taking out any of the jobs I'm working on right now.

"What's wrong?" Shen asks.

I watch him as he leans back against the wall, making himself comfortable, I'd be annoyed if any other visitor made themselves so much at home, but Shen is different. He's an easy presence. I've known him a few years, he's an orphan, like me. He came here with his mother, but she's dead now. I don't know where his father is, I've never asked. It's enough that he's a good business partner. He's okay with the scabbing, and not bad with the simple fixes. Nothing special, not near as good as me, but decent.

Where he really earns his keep is his face. He's not handsome, just an ordinary-looking boy with straight black hair that he has me hack off every few months, and skin toned closer to golden than the brown I have. The only thing memorable is those odd hazel eyes of his, but his face is ordinary, even a little goofy, with his overlarge ears. But that easy smile gets to you. People flock to the flicker of hope he carries inside him.

I know it's what drew me in. They put him on the line next to me; I was supposed to teach him how to sort. He's a year or so younger than me, and back then he'd looked it, a frightened kid, more likely to get his fingers crushed than sift out some useful scraps. I'd told him what to do and then ignored him. He'd worked beside me for a while until he was deemed trained, and then we were reshuffled.

I ignored him for years. Just like I ignore all of them. Caring for someone where you can die or be sent to a different Refuge at any time isn't worth the emotional mileage.

But he'd made some kind of an impact on me, that damn smiling face of his. Because when the light went out for a while I couldn't let things be. His mother was dead, and he was finally like the rest of us, worn down to quiet despair, and I couldn't stand it. Or maybe I just saw an opportunity. The old woman had died not long before, so I needed the help. I asked him to gather scraps for me. He latched on, and I couldn't shake him now if I tried. Not that I want to. Together we make triple what I could alone.

"Well?" he asks? "Something is going on. Did you get grief from Management for something?"

I shake my head. He's long ago negotiated with the lowest ranking Managers, something that I had never thought to do. Now they protect us from being caught.

"Not trouble, but- something happened," I tell him, "before my shift. I got taken up to see a Manager." That has his eyes widening.

"Why?"

I shrug, unwilling to say, the guilt of it choking at me. I'd accepted the offer. I'd selfishly agreed to leave him behind. But how can I tell him that?

We sit in silence, and he arranges his limbs across the hard shelf of the bunk. He reaches into his pocket.

"I have something that'll make you smile." He drops two yellow candies between us. I smile, but it pains me. Must he always share every good thing? Why can't he keep something for himself? Can't he see I'm about to betray him?

But I know from experience that he'll be hurt if I refuse, so I reach over and take one, and let the flavor, lemon he claims, dance across my tongue.

"Did you hear that they're doing a move?" he asks.

"Really? When?"

He keeps his eyes focused on the twist of plastic still in his hands. "I don't know exactly. A couple of days, I think."

For reasons no one quite understands, groups of us are shuffled around to different Refuges. This is only the second Refuge I've lived on, but others have lived on five or six. Perhaps they move the troublemakers, or maybe it's because too many babies are being born and it's getting overcrowded. Which is stupid. That problem could easily be solved by supplying birth control, but of course you can barely see a medic for a severed finger.

The Managers aren't completely evil. They don't split up married couples, or parents from young children. But there's no concession for anyone else. The only reason I'd been able to stay with the old woman was because she lied and said she was my grandmother.

"There's going to be a rush on weddings tonight though," Shen continues, and my head spins, and I hear a buzzing sound in my ears.

Could the solution be so simple? Is there a way around leaving him behind?

"We should get married," I say, before I can think it through. Would it even work? Can I save him? Or am I being selfish, trying to keep him for myself? It probably won't even work.

Shen is staring at me, looking horrified.

"You don't have to look like that," I mutter, feeling betrayed. I know we're not like that, but no one wants to see horror as the main reaction to a marriage proposal.

"That's why you got called up to see the Managers," he says. "You're being moved."

I nod, uncomfortable with the half-truth.

"I guess some of them like you enough to warn you, hey?" I nod again. I have someone looking out for me it seems.

He falls silent again, and I pull my knees up to my chest. Making myself small is a skill I've learned long ago.

"I guess we'd better get going then," Shen says, his voice catching a little, "If we want to get there before the clerk closes out the window." He shuffles of the bunk, and stands, looking back at me. He gives me a smile that's watered down from his usual. "Unless you're changing your mind?"

I shake my head resolutely and stand up beside him in the tiny dim space of the curtained alcove.

"There's just one thing," I say as he starts to turn away. He looks back, his odd eyes questioning. I look down. "No babies."

It's another reason why I have resisted any attempt to court me these last few years. With no birth control available, babies are an inevitability that I'm not willing to allow. Not here. Not in this place.

His shoulders slump a little. Sex is one of the few pleasures that we still have available. "But, you know, other things could be okay," I add, feeling my face flush. The lack of privacy in this place has ensured that we both know what other things can entail.

He surprises me by stepping closer and kissing me. A test of my willingness? I put my hands on his shoulders and kiss him back. Did he think I didn't want too? But the clock ticking away has me pulling back after a few seconds.

"We need to catch the clerk," I say, turning away from his dazed face. "Go get whatever you want to take along, we're not coming back." At least I'm not. I hope this marriage contract will be enough to ensure he won't either.

He slips out, still looking confused, and I open up the panel, taking out the only things I care about, a printed image of my family from before the war, and the neat roll of canvas containing the tools that I'd inherited from the old woman and scavenged along the way. I tuck them inside my shirt and hurry down to the clerk's office, hoping to get there ahead of the rush. Most couples go before the oldest ones to have the marriage rituals performed before coming to the clerk window to get it legally certified. I wish we had time. I wish I hadn't zombied through that shift at the belt, pretending that I was going to do anything but leave. I wish I'd had a chance to think this through better. I don't do well with snap decision making.

The line is small when I arrive, and I take a place at the end. I get curious glances from the couples in line, standing there alone and unbathed, in my usual workday rags. I didn't have time for any of that. I just hope Shen gets here before I reach the head of the line and I lose my spot. I need to be lower-level within a few hours. I avert my eyes from their looks, not wanting to see their faces lit with the hope of a new marriage. Soon enough they'll have a baby on the way and be worn down with the pain and responsibility of it. Babies die easily here. I can't let myself think about it. I will save Shen. It's all I can do. If he can be bothered to show up. What it he has changed his mind?

He makes it in time, with a bundle under his arm and a freshly washed face. I roll my eyes at him. I don't care if his face is clean or not.

The paperwork is dispensed with a quick retinal scan to confirm identity, and we're legally tied together. We can find someone to perform the rituals later.

"How long until it posts on the system?" I ask, a new worry occurring to me.

The bored low rank Manager glances at the clock. "You got some sort of rush? It posts when it posts." Her eyes shift to the couple behind us, making it clear that I'm holding up the line.

I shush Shen's questions as I rush him down levels, to the launch deck. I look at the timer on the wall. I still have an hour or so, but I don't want to be late. I need time in case I have to argue, to fight for Shen.

They scan me and pass me through, but they won't let Shen in. The fight deck is kept secure. They can't risk stowaways. I hover indecisively. Should I let them separate us in the hope that I can come back and retrieve him? It feels like the wrong choice, but the clock is ticking.

The guard looks bored, but I'm aware of the weapon at his hip. It won't do to antagonize him.

"Do we have a problem?" a cool voice questions from behind me, "I hope you're not preventing my new crew member from boarding."

I turn with relief and meet the midnight dark eyes of the Captain.

"No ma'am," the guard says, snapping to attention. "But she attempted to bring an unauthorized person through."

The Captain gives me that assessing look that so unnerved me when I first met her. Was it only this morning?

I was summoned to meet with her, woken from sleep, and lead to an upper level outside compartment. One that didn't smell like sweat and feces overlaid with wildflowers. With large windows overlooking the planet. I stood in the middle of the room, not daring to touch anything. I'd had no idea that a place this clean and lovely even existed in the filthy scrabble of a Refuge. It seemed unfair that we were packed in like insects when places like this were empty.

When the woman, with her ebony dark skin and neat uniform entered I'd started to shake. She wore authority like a right, and I wasn't sure what trouble I was in, but had to be bad.

"I'm here to offer you a job."

It was the last thing I expected her to say.

"A job?" We can't have jobs. We don't have any citizenship rights. It's why we've been shuffled from Refuge station to Refuge station for the last ten years. No planet is willing to let us in, or give us citizenship rights.

"I'm willing to sponsor you." When I still stared at her in confusion, she shook her head in annoyance. Clearly it was something I should know, and it was beneath her to explain it.

She flipped on a screen and handed it to me, and turned her back to stare out the window.

"I'll expect a full tour from you, no excuses. If you break the apprenticeship bond you will find yourself back in a Refuge station."

She looked back at me, her eyes almost angry. "I am offering you a future. Don't make me regret it."

I stood there, uncertain of what I was supposed to do. She sat down at a desk and began reading, leaving me alone with the lit screen. I looked down at the dirty smears my hands left on the pristine device. She wanted me to apprentice to her?

I read over the document, slowly. I'm one of the lucky ones. I had four years of schooling before the war came, so I can read pretty well. Now kids are lucky if their family owns a book of scripture for them to learn their letters from. There's no school here.

I'm slow to read it. I haven't had a cause to read more than a few words at a time for years.

It's a simple contract. I agree to spend the next six years bonded as apprentice mechanic, with wages that are probably paltry but seem like riches, and at the end of it I get not only my certificate of mastery, but also full citizenship in the Three Systems Union of Planets.

71

I read it a few times, but there doesn't seem to be a catch. The language is confusing in places, and it could easily have any number of catches, but why bother? I'd accept almost anything to get off this place. They could offer me lifetime slavery and I'd probably accept, as long as I had a chance to breathe real air again.

When I'm done I look up to find the important woman, Captain Andrea Lawson, according to the document, watching me.

"I trust you read the contract. Do you have any questions?"

I stare at her. She's so clean and shiny-looking.

"Why would you want me?" I'll contaminate her if come near her.

Her eyebrows go up, and she takes a sharp breath through her nose. She doesn't want to answer the question.

"You're smart and seem to have a natural skill. Why not?"

I desperately wished Shen was there to do this for me because I think too slow.

"Am I going to die from it?"

And that does shock her. "I assure you that my ship passes all workplace safety inspections. I haven't lost an employee in ten years."

I'm too tired to puzzle it out, and she softens slightly.

"There's no catch, I assure you. I have need of someone who'll work hard and not balk at spending long periods in deep space. It's hard to get apprentices to sign on for that. And you came well recommended." She looks back down at the screen on her desk. "It's a good deal, why don't you want to take it?"

I look out her window, and I can see the far edge of the other end of the Refuge, where thousands of us are getting up, going to work at jobs that are pointless and endless.

"It doesn't seem fair. I don't deserve it."

She shakes her head. "And staying here, living like this, wasting your life away, is that more fair?"

I stare at my feet. I have no answer.

"Look, I have some business to take care of here; I won't be leaving until tonight. Sign the contract, and then you can take the rest of the day, say your goodbyes. Just be on board by 2100."

I signed the contract, who wouldn't?

And then, like a zombie, I staggered off to work, going through the motions of a normal day when nothing was normal.

It's less than a day later and I'm already trying to change the terms of the contract. Perhaps she'll decide I'm too much trouble and find someone else.

"Who's this?" the Captain asks, eyeing Shen.

I gulp and take his hand. "My husband." It sounds wrong, but I pull him to stand beside me.

She shakes her head, and I'd swear that she's trying to hide a smile. "You weren't married this morning." But she doesn't try to challenge it. "How old are you boy?"

"Almost seventeen earth years."

The Captain shakes her head again and the half smile is gone. "I'm sorry. He's too young, eighteen or older is the law."

"What do you mean? I know it's legal to be married at sixteen. We haven't done anything wrong, even if I am older than him."

"I don't know what the rules are here, or among your people, but the regulation for the work we do is eighteen or older. I can't have him on board."

"He helps me with the repairs. He's smart and he works hard," I say.

"He could be the most gifted child in this system, but he would still be legally a child, and not allowed to be part of my crew."

She looks down at her device. "You still have a few minutes. I'll see you on board no later than 2100."

"Please," I beg, "there must be some way."

She sighs. "Finish your apprenticeship in good standing, gain your citizenship, and sponsor him out yourself."

"That's six years!" My voice has gone desperate and shrill, but I can't help it.

"I'm sorry," is all she says, and goes through the security gate to the launch deck beyond.

I turn back to Shen.

"I guess I'm not going anywhere after all hey?" His eyes are shiny, but he smiles anyway. "But look at you. An apprenticeship? Citizenship? It's amazing."

"I'm sorry, I'm so sorry, I thought it would be like a move, I thought she'd let us stay together."

"Don't cry," he says, and I realize that's what I'm doing. I haven't cried in years. "This is wonderful. You have a real life waiting for you, you have a future."

I should tell him that I won't go, that I'll stay with him. I can't do it. Not for Shen, not for anyone.

"I'll still be here in six years."

Will he? Life in precarious and cheap in the Refuges, no one cares if there's a few less of us. And even if he is will it all have broken him? Will he still have hope left in him?

"You don't need me, but I need you to do this. Go out there, live for both of us. You can get this marriage annulled. You know you'd never have wanted it if it wasn't for this."

He's wrong about that, about all of it. "I'm not giving up. I'll be back for you sooner rather than later." I promise myself. I will nag and beg and make the Captain come back here on his eighteenth birthday. I'll make it happen. I want to promise him, but the words stick in my throat. Instead I just pull him close for as long as we have left. And then I kiss him for the second time ever. I kiss him goodbye.

I have to strap in for takeoff, but within a few minutes the ship is flying free. I stand at a window and watch both the Refuge and the planet shrink into nothingness. The place that was my world for so long, its people, Shen, gone in a few moments. As if they'd never been there at all.

About the Author

Maree Brittenford holds certification in multiple trades. And loves writing about smart skilled women who can take care of themselves. She's the author of the Guardian trilogy, a young adult speculative fiction series. She lives in Southern California where she spends her time crafting furniture and stories.

Don't Miss an Issue!

COLOR OF THE FLAME

BY STEPHEN REID CASE

I.

There are few places more hidden than the core of a star. Its light licks off into space, but the heart of the flame remains forever unseen.

What happens in the core can be modeled, of course: the rearrangement of probabilities and affinities transmuting matter to energy. Yet anything happening a trillion times each instant at the centers of billions of stars will eventually hit a snag. Something, invariably, will go wrong. Realities will start to rub away like well-worn pennies.

Most people have faith in the stars. They know how to burn. Their particles are firm in their endless dance. The physics works.

The Godhexi knew better.

Godhex04886 monitored its star. It was an average main sequence star with a small train of planets in an especially thick section of the Milky Way. Godhex04886 had been monitoring it for over three galactic revolutions before the star threw a bad neutrino.

Godhex04886 snagged the particle in one of its eighteen-dimensional nets and coiled its manifolds with distaste.

The neutrino was sour. It had a harmonic distinctly at variance with what it should have been.

The neutrino was *wrong*.

Godhex04486 alerted the local hexametric of corresponding Godhexi. Using parameters from the sour neutrino, Godhex04486 adjusted models of the star's interior. This might be the very thing they had watched for and feared so long.

Godhex04486 ran its models again.

It had finally happened.

Godhex04486 trembled in all six of its tessellated manifolds.

According to the calculations, in a few million years the highly improbable reactions taking place in the star's core would bleed out onto its surface, curdling its flame. Godhex04486's

75

star would be the wrong color.

Not an *incorrect* color. An *impossible* color, a color that could not exist.

By now its query and subsequent ramifications had reached the local hexametric of corresponding Godhexi. A consensus was reached. It would require a vast amount of resources. It would drain the powers of the local hexametric. But it was necessary. A wrong color propagating outward into the universe was unacceptable.

This was the thing the Godhexi feared: a tipping point that would pull the whole supersaturated universe back down to the chaos of energy from which it had sprung.

The local hexametric converged.

The star would be caged.

II.

Creighton was at his letters when the alarm chimed. He skimmed the data, whistled softly, and called his wife.

"There is no way," she said. "There is absolutely no way."

"I'm just giving you the data, love." Her face hung above his desk. Behind her head, he could see the pod's curve. "And the data is pretty firm. Gravimetrics and long-range EM. Big and round and almost certainly artificial."

Chai wrinkled her nose. "Gravimetrics?"

"Yeah. You know, gravitational lensing and the proper motion of nearby objects."

"I know what it means, Creighton. You just sound like a goddamned spacer when you say it."

He held his grin for a few moments so she was sure to see it through a wash of static. "We are spacers, Chai. And this is big."

"Meaning a big payoff for you if it pans out. And a big pain in the ass for me. How far off my current trajectory?"

"Looks to be forty light years, roughly."

"I don't think I have a choice, do I?"

"Big, Chai!" Creighton threw up his hands. "Think big! Retirement big!"

"Fine, fine." She touched a few spots of light in front of her and dropped off the light line.

"Keep me posted," he said. "I'll kiss the kids goodnight."

She waved and blinked off.

Creighton shuffled his letters: real paper, facsimiles of those written by astronomers on Old Earth hundreds of year ago. He and Chai were spacers, when the situation allowed. When the situation also allowed, Creighton was an archeologist of sorts.

The letters were correspondence from when stars could only be studied visually and only through distorting layers of atmosphere and glass lenses.

The batch he had now was between observers discussing variable stars. One of them had published nearly five hundred years ago a catalogue of red stars in which their shades were reported in descriptions as lovely as they were unquantifiable. It was a hobby of his, though occasionally the letters offered leads useful leads.

"It's a Dyson sphere, Creighton." Chai's face blinked back above the desk. "It's a motherfucking Dyson sphere."

"The kids are downstairs. There's a small but not vanishing possibility they'll hear you."

"They've got to learn to talk someday."

Numbers and video-feed streamed beside her. Her eyes were on her screens, outside his line of sight.

"Do you want me to flag Central?"

"I've already done it," she said. "I've got a few survey blips dropped. We'll get a good cut for this, you were right. There hasn't been a genuine ETI haul for, what?"

"Six months."

"And maybe never anything so large. They'll be all over this."

"How large?"

He waited for her answer.

"Gods, I don't know," she finally said. "I mean, I do. You've got the numbers there. But getting that in your mind is something else. How big is it?"

He studied the figures now gliding past. "At least thirteen light-minutes."

"That's, like, a system, right?"

"You could hold a star and a small train of planets inside, yes. What does it look like?"

"Black," she said. "Absolutely black. Trusses on the outside, like a geodesic dome. But each one a million miles long or something. I'm going to run a light line around it."

"You've already flagged it. We'll get our cut."

"Yeah." She leaned off screen for a moment. "But now I want to see it. See the other side. This is crazy."

She blinked off again.

Central loved artifacts of clear extra-terrestrial intelligence. They would take all they could find, whether unprotected ruins on one of the Granite Worlds or additional dreadnoughts from the Cocoon Fleet. Problem was, after the finders got a cut, Central clamped down tight. In another few hours the whole system would likely be quarantined.

And Chai wanted to nose around first.

He shrugged and went back to his letters. This correspondence hadn't been linked to Chai's trajectory, but on a hunch he put the physical copies aside and shifted through them as data files. He filtered historical stellar maps and correlated them with the estimated location of this object as seen from Old Earth half a millennium ago, then cross-referenced that with his letters. Two seconds later he had something:

My dear Sir John,

I can with satisfaction inform you of the diligence with which I have been pursuing your suggestion to study the heavens for deep red stars. Your remarks have led me to the conclusion that such objects are indeed likely to be variable, and after some nights of observations I am led to the same conclusion which you presented in your *Treatise*: namely that dim red stars are variable and tend moreover to develop a *nebulous* haze about them at their period of greatest diminution.

I offer one remarkable example of this phenomenon. The star noted in your charts at the following coordinates, I observed over the course of several nights and found to be rapidly decreasing in brightness. By the end of a fortnight, I could no longer locate it. Before it had decreased beyond the range of sensibility, however, I was keenly aware that it seemed to take on a diffuse and--if you will excuse the imprecise description--hairy or foggy characteristic. I have turned my instruments on these coordinates for several nights since but have not been able to detect any further indication of its presence.

Do you know whether this particular star has exhibited periodicity in the past and if so when I might expect it to return to visibility? If I have made a new discovery, I would be obliged to you for its communication to the Astronomical Society at their next meeting, as personal obligations make it unlikely I will be able to travel to London in time for the next meeting.

I remain your humble servant.

Creighton slapped the meta-wood desk.

It had been observed. Someone in the distant past on Old Earth had witnessed a star being netted over by an ETI of planetary-engineering capacity.

Of stellar-system-engineering capacity.

He blinked his wife. "It was observed from Earth."

"What was?"

"The Dyson sphere. The *building* of the Dyson sphere. There was a dim red star there five hundred years ago--longer actually, allowing light travel time. And some English gentleman *witnessed* it being contained. Encapsulated. Whatever."

"What's an English?" She was distracted.

"Never mind. But it means there was ETI activity in that area as recently as within a millennium. That makes it even hotter."

"More money?"

"If we can link it to a specific temporal event, you bet more money. And it looks like I just did." A chime sounded from downstairs, and Creighton rose. "That's the kids. I've got to go. Get as much info as you can. It's bigger than we thought."

"You said it was retirement big."

"Bigger than that. If this pans out, I'm buying you a second body."

She orbited the Dyson sphere. No one from Central had showed up yet, which was fine. The flag she dropped was buzzing on all frequencies, so there was no chance they'd contest the find when they arrived.

There wasn't much to see of the sphere beyond a round immensity, like someone had put a lid over all the stars in one direction. The trusses supporting it were barely visible in starlight.

It was not completely black though. It wasn't radiant in the visible portion of the electromagnetic spectrum, but it was glowing faintly in microwaves.

"It does have a star inside," Chai mused. "Assumedly. So the sphere around it would eventually heat up. Assumedly."

She told the pod to run some numbers. How long would it take a star's radiation to heat its cage to luminosity?

"What's it made of?" she asked the pod.

A feed of information flowing down her screens highlighted and magnified. The sphere appeared to be mainly carbon and silicon.

She blinked her husband back. "What did you say about the kind of star this was? Someone on Old Earth saw it?"

"All I know is that it appeared to be a dim red star in the historical record. Why?"

"It's glowing."

"Huh." He pulled at his beard. "I guess that makes sense, given enough time."

"The pod says in a few million years it will be glowing in the visible portion of the spectrum. Imagine that. A star inside a star."

He said "Huh" again.

"Odd." She looked at the screen. "That's really bizarre."

"What?"

"When it starts glowing. Heated up long enough by the presumed star inside. When it start to glow."

"Yes?"

"It will be the wrong color."

Godhex04934—a later iteration of Godhex04886—awoke and glanced toward the shielded sun, wondering what had brought it out of stasis. There was a flicker of non-relativistic motion in orbit. Someone was knocking on the door.

Godhex04934 sent a targeted warning on all frequencies.

"Danger. Do not approach the cage."

"I'm sorry," Creighton said. "I lost you there for a second. There was some kind of interference."

"I said it will be the wrong color."

"What do you mean?"

"Given long enough, it will start to glow."

"Right."

"And it will be glowing the wrong color."

"The wrong color?" Creighton asked. "What does that even mean?"

"It means--" She paused. "It will be a color no one has seen before."

She was an artist, and she had an imagination. But even with the most up-to-date packages integrated into her cortex, Chai sometimes did things with numbers Creighton couldn't explain.

"Look, I'm assuming you've run the black body equations, and that they're showing the shell will start radiating after enough heat has been absorbed from its internal star."

"Yeah." She stared at him. "Duh."

"So its frequency--its color--is going to depend on temperature."

"No."

"What do you mean?"

"Just what I said. Here, I'll send you the numbers."

He waited. They did not come.

"Well?"

"Hold on." There was another burst of static. "There's someone here."

It looked like a snowflake: six sides, with filigreed edges trailing off into fractal structures too small to follow. None of the equipment on the pod registered it. She couldn't see where it had come from.

"ETI," she said. "In the flesh. Hot damn."

Creighton was saying something, but she couldn't make out the words. In another instant all the screens went blank.

The snowflake seemed small, perhaps a few feet across, but sizes were notoriously difficult to judge in the black. It might have been a hundred meters away, in which case it would be much larger. It was definitely keeping pace between her and the sphere.

Her pod began vibrating. Words formed, not on a screen but shaped in the air of the pod itself.

"Do not approach the cage," it said.

She was suddenly frightened. What was taking those ships from Central so long? There had been reports of exchanges with ETIs in the past, and they usually ended in derelict vessels and insane crews. She tapped the controls tentatively, trying to edge away.

"Do not approach the cage."

They spun together in silence. After several minutes, Chai's fear gave way to impatience.

"What is it?" she asked. "What's inside?"

"It is a cage," the voice said. "It is isolating the star within."

"Why?"

"The star is an impossible color. It must remain isolated."

"It won't for much longer. That shell's been absorbing heat for centuries. Eventually it'll start to glow."

The snowflake winked. At least, the central node of the six fractal-like fins sparked momentarily.

The pod's controls came back online.

Chai fled.

Godhex04934 turned away from the vessel and considered the cage's surface. It was impossible this outcome was not predicted. The star's electromagnetic output was mapped and projected. How could something as simple as the absorption and reabsorption of its contaminant radiation have been overlooked? The larger hexametric would not have allowed such a simple oversight.

Godhex04934 shuddered down to the hyper-dimensional tips of its countless flagella.

This was evidence of the breakdown represented by the impossible color itself. The corrosion of reality and probability within the star apparently had implications for the central processing units of the local hexametric itself.

They had made a mistake.

Godhex04934 communed with all surrounding Godhexi, and these in turn linked themselves into the higher iteration of hexametrics, until the eyes of the entire galactic hexameron were turned upon the problem of this widening contamination.

The local hexameron converged on the star once more.

III.

Chai and Creighton had only ten children. It was all they could afford before their big ETI find. By the time they made it big, their brooding license had expired. They did move to one of the new glassworlds though, in a tight orbit around a bright crystalline white dwarf. She devoted her time to her art and he spent the rest of his career sifting through his facsimile historical artifacts.

Their youngest daughter eventually went to work for Central, serving several years before being posted to a listening station near the Black Pearl.

"At least, that's what we call it," the training ensign told her when she boarded the circling station. "The Snowflakes are class one ETI, the only class one yet detected. They keep adding layers to the Pearl, like a mussel does a piece of grit. Did you ever see a mussel?"

The daughter, whose name was Huldah, shook her head. She stared beyond the transparent viewers to where tiny spots of light crossed in front of the black sphere.

"They're sucking material from the cores of about a dozen nearby red giants, best we can tell," the ensign explained. He was thin, with the blue skin of one of the early ring worlds. "Of course we don't know how they do it. They won't let us get close enough to see. But they keep a constant stream of it weaving around that thing. Since we've been watching, they've completed the second shell, leaving about half a standard AU in between it and the first."

"It's a Dyson sphere," Huldah said.

"Right. But now doubled: a sphere around a sphere. And they keep at it."

"No contact?"

"They're not talking. They don't have to. They're class one. We can't get any closer than they want us to."

"What are they like?"

The ensign pointed to a terminal. "The entire database is there. You'll have plenty of time to read up while you watch the Pearl."

Huldah knew this place. Its discovery had been the highpoint of her parents' careers. Her father used to talk about it.

"A red star. Known to amateur observers," he would say with a sort of hushed awe. "Seeing ETI at work with no idea."

The stories her mother told were stranger. She began painting in earnest after they moved to the glassworld. She was trying to capture something, she said. Something she had caught a glimpse of in the equations from the Dyson sphere.

A color that could not be seen.

"Why not?" she mused, staring at the Pearl.

"Because the universe is supersaturated." A Snowflake materialized in front of her. It looked just as her mother had described, its size impossible to judge. "We have seen your kind before. The wrong color is the color of decay. Or of flame. Flame is a falling, in a sense, correct?"

Huldah stared.

"Apologies for the language. We have been listening to the listeners." The Snowflake paused. "Am I clear?"

Huldah nodded.

"Flame is a falling. It is a system moving from a higher state of energy to lower. Once flame begins, the entire system falls into it. The universe is likewise a system. My words still are clear?"

Again, a mute nod.

"My words are clear. The caged star contains a flame. It is a place where the universe begins falling. It does this in an impossible physical manifestation."

"You built the Dyson sphere."

"Correct." The oscillating waves of color on the Snowflake's edges were hypnotic. Huldah kept trying to follow them to their endpoints and failing. "But we omitted basic thermodynamic principles, inexplicably. We began constructing multiple shields. We are delaying the collapse of this crystalline universe for billions of years."

"Why are you telling me this?"

"So you will know."

There were Snowflakes all around her. On the screens she could see them materializing outside as well.

"We discover evidence of the collapse along unforeseen vectors," the Snowflake continued. "This troubles us. It is possible there is peripheral contamination."

They were spreading thin streams of a black ribbon, darker than the dark of space. It was another shell, she realized. It would envelope the listening station.

"Perhaps it came from the one who was similar to you," the Snowflake said. "She saw the equations, but

you--"

The Snowflake had vanished, but its voice remained.

"You dream an impossible color."

It was correct. Huldah did and always had. But how do you communicate knowledge of a color no one has seen?

Huldah looked toward the Black Pearl and imagined she saw its surface glowing.

She waited.

About the Author

Stephen Reid Case teaches and researches on the history of astronomy. His stories and reviews have appeared in Strange Horizons, Beneath Ceaseless Skies, Daily Science Fiction, and elsewhere. His novel, First Fleet, is available from Axiomatic Publishing, and his monograph on the astronomy of Sir John Herschel (research that inspired the story appearing here) is forthcoming from University of Pittsburgh Press.

You can find him online at www.stephenreidchase.com or on Twitter @BoldSaintCroix.

Now Available
from all your favorite booksellers
in trade paper and electronic editions

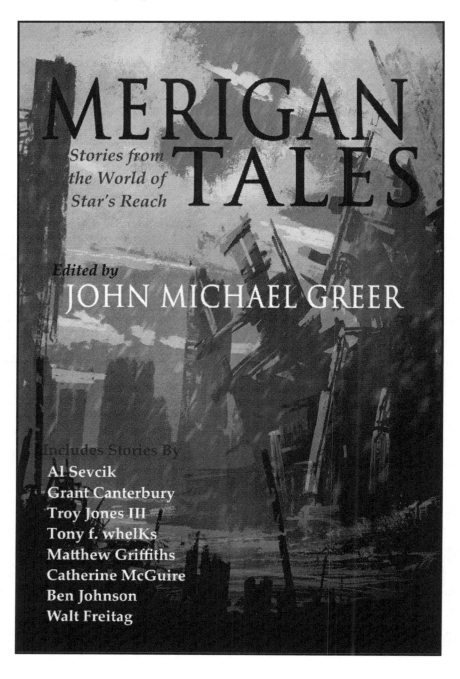

MERIGAN TALES

Stories from the World of Star's Reach

Edited by

JOHN MICHAEL GREER

Includes Stories By
Al Sevcik
Grant Canterbury
Troy Jones III
Tony f. whelKs
Matthew Griffiths
Catherine McGuire
Ben Johnson
Walt Freitag

IN BUSINESS TO SERVE AND PROTECT

BY GREGG CHAMBERLAIN

"Hello. Are you ready for the end of the world?"

An earnest smile plastered across his face, the charming young man on the screen vanished. In his place appeared archival news footage of the Hawaii Meteor just moments before an aerial assault involving a combination of the Demolition Man's force beams, Lady Freedom's sonic shockwave battle cry, and the mysterious Mensa's psychokinetic pulse blew it into a harmless shower of cosmic dust and pebbles raining all over the island chain, leaving behind millions of expensive and deep dents in state highway pavements and urban sidewalks along with more than a few shattered residential slate-tile roofs. The young man reappeared on-screen, gazing with calculated caring and concern at his audience.

"Is your business, office, or other place of work covered in case of collateral damage during a climactic confrontation between Good and Evil?"

El Monstro and the New York Giant now appeared on the screen, smashing and crashing around Times Square in their recent epic fight-to-the-finish. Chunks of concrete from shattered buildings rained down like cannonball-sized hailstones, landing with devastating effect on the roofs of cars, buses and trucks wedged together in an impassable traffic jam, except for where the feet of the two gargantuan combatants had flattened out openings. Showers of glass from broken windows and electronic billboard signs surrounding the square shattered into splintered shrapnel on the sidewalks as panic-stricken tourists and locals struggled to flee via any available exit.

"Does your family health plan provide you with adequate protection against alien symbiont infestation, rage viral outbreak, or globe-spanning plagues of Biblical proportion?"

Dead-eyed people shambled across the screen in pursuit of fleeing victims until enveloped in a sudden green cloud spewing from the nozzles of backpack spray guns in the hands of the Repo Man and Scarletina, who sheltered behind one of Finn M'Cool's trademark icicle-fence barriers. The living zombie horde emerged from the gas cloud, everyone shaking their heads and blinking their eyes with returning awareness.

"Is your personal security system adequate defence against mutant mobs, tech-enhanced burglars, or other-dimensional home invaders?"

Gated community security cam footage showed the vague outline of Shadow Stalker slipping out of a residence through a closed front door, right into a phantom punch courtesy of the Guardian Ghost.

"Will your travel insurance safeguard you against devil doctors and their demonic death traps or eldritch entities in search of a few good souls to snack on?"

The Diabolist leered at the struggling form of a naked voluptuous woman (her chest area digitally masked on screen), bound with silver chains to a blood-stained onyx altar even as he raised overhead a stone sacrificial knife, unholy glyphs glow-

ing along its chipped edge. A blinding beam of light knocked the satanic sorcerer out of view of the camera. Myrddin the Magnificent appeared in his place, pausing for but a moment to cast his own star-spattered cloak over the almost-victim's prone form, covering her nakedness, before he hurled a miniature lightning bolt in the Diabolist's direction.

"If you are a client of Consolidated Assurance and Protection for Emergencies Ltd., the obvious answer is 'Yes'."

Oozing with empathy, the young man reappeared, seated behind a large and impressive-looking desk/computer work station. In back of him on a huge plasma-display screen, Myrddin the Magnificent released the shaken near-victim of the Diabolist from the altar chains and escorted her to safety. Fading in to replace that scene appeared the logo for Consolidated Assurance and Protection for Emergencies Ltd., with the letters C.A.P.E. in big, bold red relief against a blue-and-white background. Speaking in a tone of convincing conviction, the young man carried on.

"Other insurance agencies can deal with the ordinary problems of fire, flood, and Acts of God. But only C.A.P.E. Ltd. can handle the hazards of living in the real world of metahuman mistakes, mutant menaces, and miraculous mischief."

Behind the young man's caring face, the C.A.P.E. logo faded away into a fast-moving montage: white-coated researchers laboured in laboratories; trimly-muscled men and women worked out, with and without weapons or powers, in training gyms; a circle of robed men and women, of varying ages, sat in meditation, lotus-fashion, in an austere Zen garden; a quick succession of cameo shots then followed of a variety of rooms ranging from weapons lockers to cavernous archival storage vaults.

"Drawing on years and years and years of years of experience, C.A.P.E. Ltd. employs a team of experts drawn from the most renowned ranks in the realms of super science, along with the greatest gonzo gimmicks of gearhead gadgeteer freelance contractors. Our trained field agents are ready to use all their skills, strengths and superpowers to shield you and your loved ones from harm. We also have on 24-hour alert a myriad of masters and mistresses of the mystic arts who will manage any and all malevolent mages making magical mayhem along with their mad monstrous minions."

The young man and his desk/computer station vanished from view again. The wall screen zoomed forward and displayed a scene of giant construction robots morphing into action to sort through and clear away building rubble while android medics perform triage on victims. The suasive monologue continued.

"Our specially-engineered automaton armada also stands by in reserve to rebuild and restore cities and societies, and to repair and rectify any damage to person and property."

The screen froze on the image of a sleeping baby, wrapped in a silver space blanket, cradled in the protective arms of an impressive-looking android nurse. The camera view pulled back to again present the smiling young man now seated at the front of his desk.

"Every C.A.P.E. customer can rest assured and sleep easy at night knowing that the nabobs of the nether realms are nullified and the multiverse is made safe for truth, justice, and every individual's right to pursue personal happiness. We here at Consolidated Assurance and Protection for Emergencies Ltd. are always available and ever ready to welcome new clients."

Behind him, the scene on the wall screen switched to a call centre cubicle where a young woman, seated in front of a computer, glanced to her left at a glowing crystal ball, before turning her attention back to her computer as she tapped a few keys.

"Our telemarketing sales staff of cybernetically-enhanced psionicists and praeternaturally-amped psychics have already calculated all the myriad probabilities and possibilities for your membership agreement, and also recorded in advance, as a precaution, all your personal and financial details, thus allowing our advanced-Ultra A.I. Auditor to assign you to your correct actuarial account. All that they require to activate your account is a real-time/space continuum acceptance from you."

Standing up, the young man flashed a sincere smile as he walked around the desk and seated himself again. Hands folded together in a convincing and conclusive attitude, he leaned in towards the viewer, his eyes expanding into a captivating stare.

"So say 'Yes' and avoid becoming just another one of the horde of frantic ones marching merrily in blissful ignorance toward an oblivious and uncaring apocalypse. Act now and step within the shelter of C.A.P.E. Ltd. Be part of the Consolidated Assurance and Protection for Emergencies Ltd. family preferred clients. Wear your C.A.P.E. status with pride and be the first in your neighbourhood to shout out the sacred word that will identify you as being among the Fearless Ones."

The C.A.P.E. Ltd. logo reappeared behind the earnest young man as the camera viewpoint receded to show him throwing up both hands in the air in Nixon-esque "V" for Victory signs.

"Excelsior!"

There was an audible click and the triumphant image froze on the screen. The Chairman of the Board took his hand away from the built-in armrest remote control panel. The assembled directors of the board of Consolidated Assurance and Protection for Emergencies Ltd. turned their attention away from the wall-sized view screen towards the head of the boardroom table.

"So then, ladies and gentlemen," the Chairman said, scanning the two dozen directors, most dressed in conservative business suits while others affected more casual attire, although a very few wore their alter-ego uniforms, complete to masks and cowls, "I believe this concludes the presentation of our upcoming new public promotion campaign, all part of the global launch for Consolidated Assurance and Protection for Emergencies Ltd. We are on schedule for official openings of C.A.P.E. Ltd. branch offices in every major urban centre, including capital cities, throughout Europe, Asia, Africa, Australia, and South America. I think it is safe to say that within a year, at the very most, they will be as profitable as our North American network branches have proven."

The Chairman paused for a moment to remove a set of sound-baffling ear pods. The board members did the same, everyone placing their pods in small receptacles built into the oakwood table top. The sole exceptions were the Doom Knight and Death Knight, the sibling twins relying on the built-in aural protection systems of their power armour to safeguard them from any and all subliminal audio influences.

"Now," said the Chairman, folding massive, manicured hands in front of him on the table, "let us move on to the 'Questions of the Day' portion of the meeting. Yes, Dr. Praetorius?"

The elderly vulture-faced board member lowered his hand. "What are the projections," he hissed, "on potential profit margins?"

The Chairman smiled in return and tapped a key on his chair's control pad. He waved towards the wall screen and the zooming-in close-up of the sincere smiling features of the C.A.P.E. Ltd. commercial spokesman. "Based on the results of a beta-group sample test," he answered, "I rather suspect that our Mr. Parsons, an apprentice employee of exceptional and unique ability, will soon provide us

all, along with the major shareholders and even those with mere common stock portfolios, with very sizeable dividends in the next quarter's return, and a possible stock split at year's end. I also expect that Prince Charming, as Mr. Parsons is listed in his personnel file, will soon see promotion to journeyman status with a very nice Christmas bonus also as a reward for his efforts."

The Doom Knight rapped an armoured fist for attention against the table top. The Chairman suppressed an instinctive wince at the knuckle-shaped dent in the oakwood surface and signed for the other to speak. "What is the breakdown," rasped the Doom Knight's electronically-altered voice, "on the promotional strategy? It may be persuasive, but is it pervasive?"

The Chairman resisted the urge for a sarcastic retort. "You will all find in your confidential email files a folder labelled It's Your Turn To Smile. Inside is a report from MalShare Ltd., one of our most reliable independent contractors, with a complete summary of the marketing plan, both through standard newspaper, radio and television services, as well as electronic and traditional billboard ads. There is an extensive e-commerce strategy through the C.A.P.E. Ltd. website plus the usual network of social media sites, along with the customary Dark Web links. It is, of course, S.O.P. virus-proofed with a code-embedded 'bloodhound' tracker to trace back any hacking attempts and deal with the perpetrator in the approved summary fashion."

The Chairman grinned. "Please also note the proposed expansion of our clientele base. No longer will the services of Consolidated Assurance and Protection for Emergencies Ltd. be limited to national and metropolitan governments, major corporate and multinational businesses, Fortune 500 clientele, or public and private security services with secret "slush fund" budgets. No, ladies and gentlemen, soon C.A.P.E. Ltd. policies will be made available to Everyman, thanks to a sliding scale premiums system from the Auditor. Those who can pay more, will pay more while those who cannot pay much will pay what they can on the natural expectation that *someone* will come when they call for help. Barring any outside interference, of course, from a registered protector like Titan or freelancer such as the Mist."

Dr. Praetorius cocked his head, like a buzzard surveying a corpse. "And will someone respond?"

"Of course," replied the Chairman. "Perhaps not one of our A-list agents, perhaps, but a C.A.P.E. Ltd. client can always depend on receiving aid, of some sort, even if only a Class C investigator."

The Chairman smiled and nodded in acknowledgement of the appreciative chuckles and titters from the directors. "Well, even our rookie agents need some kind of field training if they hope to advance as sidekicks and minions."

The Death Knight turned a skull-faced armoured head towards the head of the table. "Can we depend" asked a sepulchral monotone, "on the current crises and catastrophes carrying on around the world?"

The Chairman offered a reassuring smile. "With international affairs as they are now—and let us be grateful for old-style dictators and their sabre-rattling showmanship—along with the still-vibrant activities of organized crime and any number of terrorist and public militia groups, I am sure that none of us need be concerned for our retirement portfolios. But, if global conditions were to quiet down, HR can always offer up a manufactured disaster or concoct a crimewave or two."

Steepling his fingers, the Chairman looked up and down the length of the table. "Now, unless there are further queries—no?—then I should like to call the question. Those in favour of launching the new campaign? Those against? The motion is carried, unanimous."

The Chairman stood up and bowed. "Thank you, ladies and gentlemen. This meeting of the Board of Directors of Consolidated Assurance and Protection for Emergencies Ltd. is adjourned, if I might have a seconder—thank you, Red Widow—and now let us retire to the next room where we shall enjoy an excellent buffet and toast the continued success of C.A.P.E. Ltd. I understand there are several bottles of a very nice Rothschild along with a selection of imported beers for those whose taste does not run to champagne."

A Cheshire Cat-like smile spread across the Chairman's face. "I don't know about the rest of you but I'm feeling very optimistic about this year. There's never been a better time to be in the business of protecting and serving the public. And at a handsome profit too."

About the Author

By day, **Gregg Chamberlain** is a mild-mannered senior-aged reporter for a mighty community newspaper. But, in actual fact, he is SuperScribe! Faster than a looming deadline! More powerful than a pontificating politician! Able to leap any obstacle to get to the story! With his spouse, best friend and confidant, Anne, and their clowder of cats, Gregg rises every day for a relentless battle in the name of Truth, Justice, and...the Canadian Way (which involves at least an extra-large box of timbits), pursuing his dream of Big Name Writer with stories in Mythic, Apex, Weirdbook, Pulp Literature and other magazines, and online at Daily Science Fiction, and in a variety of anthologies.

FOUNDERS HOUSE PUBLISHING

Independent Publishers Of Genre Fiction, Nonfiction, And Select Anthologies

Visit us at www.foundershousepublishing.com

The *Inter States* Series:

What if America failed to decisively turn away from fossil-fuel dependence when it still had the capital and geopolitical security to do so?

What if the disappearance of America's middle class became a permanent condition, and, along with it, the disappearance of national popular democracy in all by name only?

What if the effects of climate change started to significantly affect U.S. politics and economics?

"Crisp, fast-paced, and uncomfortably plausible....a new series set in a crumbling, dysfunctional United States in the not too distant future. Readers who want something more interesting and challenging than one more helping of yesterday's futures will find Meima's narrative well worth their time."

-John Michael Greer

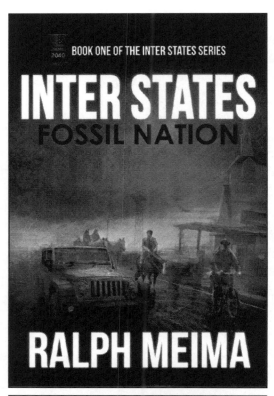

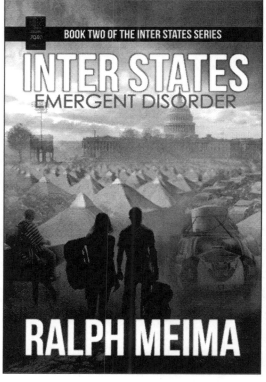

ALEXANDER HAMILTON SEES THE FUTURE

BY NATHANIEL WEBB

As I am soon to die, I have decided to put down this story, true or not. I may be the last man alive who knows the tale: my father told it to me only once, near the end of his own life; I do not know if he ever told it to my siblings, and I certainly never passed it on to my own children. Therefore, despite my misgivings about the effect the act may have on my father's place in history and public esteem, I shall tell it.

I ask only that you hold in a most sacred trust the following inalienable fact: my father, Alexander Hamilton, first president of the United States of Columbia, was not a madman.

The story, as my father told it, began on the evening of October 13th, 1781. You may place this date during the Siege of Yorktown, and indeed, the tale concerns the events of the decisive day of that battle, October 14th.

But let me not get ahead of myself. On the evening of the 13th, Lieutenant Colonel Alexander Hamilton was polishing his boots in a private command tent some 150 yards from the Albian line. His battalion of light infantry were checking their rifles and fixing their bayonets down in the trenches ahead of him, and all seemed set for the next day's assault on the Albian redoubts not far from their position. It was in this moment of quiet before battle that the extraordinary events occurred.

All at once there was a flash of bluish light in the center of the tent. Hamilton's first thought was of an Albian grenade, but there had been no sound, no flame, no concussion—only light. As his eyes cleared, Hamilton saw that the flash had resolved itself into a sort of ball of blue-white lightning, like St. Elmo's fire or a discharge from an electrical battery. Wondering at this spectacle, he began backing towards the flap of his tent, still uncertain if this were all some desperate Albian assault.

As Hamilton reached the exit, eyes still fixed on the crackling will-o-wisp before him, he saw it begin to change. It grew, slowly, and as it grew it took form; as the light grew, so too did a sort of rushing sound, like a far-off river. First the light made a sort of outline; next it seemed to resolve into individual electrical arcs that leapt from point to point on a most impressive contraption that fit the vague outline of the glow.

Here I must say that my father's descriptions to me were vague at best, but the form he described was of a sort of open-topped two-seater carriage, without wheels, but surrounded instead by a panoply of hydraulic pistons, all pumping and roaring as if they would burst apart at any moment. At the foot of the carriage was a large metal box, from which the arc lightning seemed to leap, though these emanations were already dying away.

Warm steam now seemed to fill the room, as though the great machine were breathing a dying breath, for indeed the roar of the pistons shrank to a low hum, rose suddenly to a fierce whine, then stopped all at once like the screaming of a woman who has had a firm hand clamped over her mouth. Small sparks and lightnings seemed to jump within the steam clouds for a moment, then all cleared, and before Hamilton stood the impossible machine described above.

In the seat of the carriage sat two persons of a most unusual, to Hamilton's eyes, appearance. The one who first caught his attention was a most handsome young woman, perhaps sixteen years of age, who was writing furiously in a small, leather-bound notebook. She wore a khaki bush jacket; a matching bowler hat, adorned with a pair of brass-and-leather goggles, barely kept her wavy brown hair in check. The clothes were well-fitted to her small, ladylike frame, bespeaking both money and a sense of style. She hardly looked up but went right back to her scribbling, clearly taking down all she observed with her bright, intelligent brown eyes.

Of the lady's companion, his most striking feature was his beard, which extended well down his chest and retained a sort of dirty-blond color below his lips, but deepened to a rich chestnut brown where it sprouted from his cheeks and mustache. Thinning hair on top revealed a high, intelligent forehead; buried under the beard and the middle-age were the remains of a very handsome, sensitive-faced man. His clothing and top-hat, while well-fitted, were of no great worth or notability.

"Good God!" he cried. "It worked! Florrie, look up, girl!"

"Oh, Max, hush!" the young woman replied. "I'm *observing*."

The bearded man, clearly having been stunned by his own arrival, only now saw Alexander Hamilton standing before him, looking pale as a sheet and about as ready to blow away.

"My lord! You're not—are you?" cried the bearded man, staring intently at Hamilton as he began to rise from the seat of his machine. "Where are we?"

The sight of the stranger beginning to approach him snapped Hamilton back into mindfulness and action.

"Keep yourself there, sir, while you explain how you came to be here, and why!" Stepping towards the newcomers, Hamilton put a hand to his saber.

"My name, sir, is James Clerk Maxwell," replied the stranger, removing his hat with the utmost respect. "And you, sir, if I may be so bold, are Alexander Hamilton."

"The president?!" cried the young girl, Florrie, her head snapping up for the first time.

"President?" asked Hamilton.

"No, Florrie, no!" said Maxwell, turning to look down at his companion. "I shouldn't even have said his name, damn fool that I am!"

"He is so!" retorted Florrie. She stood up with the grace of a queen, and doffed her little bowler just like a gentleman. "And I, sir, if I may be so bold, sir, am the Lady Florence Douglas, sir. And I am well honored to be in the presence of the father of the United States."

Alexander Hamilton stood statue-like for a long moment, and then he laughed, one short, dismissive bark.

"So! You are touched, the both of you, however you came to my tent. I am president of nothing save my battalion, young lady. There is nothing to be president of, not yet, although we'll see what the redcoats have to say about it tomorrow evening."

"1781!" cried Maxwell suddenly.

"It is, sir," said Hamilton with all seriousness, turning back to the older gentleman. "Had you forgotten?"

Just then two infantrymen pushed through the flaps of the tent, bayonets gleaming on the ends of their rifles.

"We heard noise, sir!" said the first of them.

"Is it spies, Colonel?" asked the second, advancing eagerly, point-first.

"No, sir, wait, I beg you!" said Maxwell. "Permit us to explain who we are, and how we came to be here."

"Why?" replied Hamilton.

"Let 'em explain it to the lash," said the second infantryman.

"Or the rope," added the first, stepping near to the young girl.

"Because—because, damn my fool heart, I can offer you a glimpse of your future history as first president of the United States of Columbia."

Hamilton raised a hand, and his soldiers stopped their advance. The forward one dropped a heavy hand on Florrie's shoulder.

"That won't be necessary, Ross. You both may step just outside, thank you." The two soldiers shared a worried look, but obeyed.

"Now speak," said Hamilton to Maxwell, "and make it clear and brief. I have much to do."

"Thank you, sir," replied Maxwell. "Let me begin by explaining that our arrival here was something of a planned accident, if you take my meaning. I have been deep in experimentation at my laboratory in Cambridge, where, having unraveled the tangled threads of matter's laws, I had dived headlong and swum in the dark waters of time's mysteries. I mean to say that I am a physicist, mathematician, and sometime mechanical, and I do believe I have invented the first machine for the traveling of time."

"You mean you are not from 1781," said Hamilton slowly, "but rather travelled here from some other year."

"1871, in fact!" said Florrie brightly. "We chose a simple anagram, see?"

"Though you've offered no explanation," replied Hamilton, "of how from Cambridge you came to the colonies."

"I wondered that myself," replied Maxwell, "but now I believe I understand. You know the earth orbits the sun at a rate of one revolution per year. Though it travels time quite neatly, my machine is not mobile in the regular sense, and this means that if I were to travel back or forward to any date not measurable in complete years from my starting date, I would find myself hanging in the ether of space, having what I must believe would be a most novel experience, whatever it was. Now no doubt my calculations were off, accounting as I had to for slight variations in the earth's orbit, and so we were deposited in your tent in Yorktown, Virginia, rather than at the Cavendish lab back in Cambridge."

"I see," said Hamilton uncertainly. "Now, then—"

"But all in all, I think, not bad for a first try!" interrupted Florrie. "Now then, let's finish with the formalities, shall we? We must prove to you that we are not mad, and so must ply you with personal facts of a sort only revealed to the public after a man's death, and only heeded by the public when the man in question was very famous or very infamous. So, to my history books!"

With that cry on her lips, Florrie turned her back to Hamilton. Maxwell stepped carefully off the machine, now fingering his beard with a most contemplative look on his face. Lifting the seat of the carriage, Florrie peered down and then dipped in a quick hand, coming back up with a slender book labelled "The Columbian Revolution, 1776-1781."

"Here we go!" she said joyously, finding a page near the end of the book. "'Hamilton, Alexander. Born the island of Nevis, January 11th, 1755 or 1757.' Oh, that's not a good start."

"1757, thank you, young lady," replied Hamilton absentmindedly. He had seen the impossible already; the explanation offered by the two strangers, their strange accents and clothes, the book the young girl held... all fit together, almost too easily.

"Here's the good stuff," Florrie went on. "'Born out of wedlock'—oh, dear—'born out of wedlock to Rachel Faucett Lavien and James A. Hamilton. In 1750 Lavien left her first husband, Johann Michael Lavien, and first son, on the island of St. Croix, and escaped to St. Kitts...' and so on... 'denied an education by the Church of Albion for his bastard status... abandoned by his father, mother died 1768 of fever, adopted by Peter Lytton until Lytton's suicide...' Oh, Mr. President, I'm sorry! I had no idea!"

Throughout the recitation Hamilton's face had been reddening. Now he straightened his back and said through clenched teeth, "And of my presidency, please?"

"Now, sir—" began Maxwell.

"I'm certain you can find every reason not to tell me, is that so? Perhaps because it has not yet happened, unlike those personal facts you've somehow dug up?"

"Very well," said Maxwell, sounding very tired. He took the book from Florrie's hands and turned a page. "Tomorrow you shall distinguish yourself in the taking of the Albian redoubt number ten. This fame shall bring you to the public eye, and lead to a distinguished career in politics, culminating in your acclamation as the first president of the United States of Columbia in 1789, followed by unanimous reelection in 1792 and 1796."

"Redoubt ten?" laughed Hamilton. "Not likely. Lafayette's aide, de Gimat, is leading that particular assault. And good luck to him, I might add; I am not much inclined to die in the last days of a won war." Now, at last, he turned toward the tent's opening, making to summon his guards.

"Please, sir!" cried Maxwell. "You must fight this battle; you must lead this assault!"

"Who are you to give me orders?" cried Hamilton, turning on his stockinged heel. "I am a Lieutenant Colonel in the Continental Army, recently aide to General Washington. You are no one at best, a madman at all odds, and a damned spy at worst!"

"All I can do, sir, is beg," said Maxwell quietly.

"Beg 'til your knees wear thin, Mister Maxwell. Tomorrow I shall watch as Lieutenant Colonel de Gimat leads my men to his glory, and tomorrow when the war is over I shall fade back into obscurity. Now then, if you are travelers in time, as you say, then prove it. Take your machine back and away from here. It will both prove your story and save you a harsher interrogation at the hands of my men."

Maxwell stood a while in thought, but finally turned away from Hamilton. "Very well, sir," he said. "Florrie—"

"No!" cried the girl.

"Florrie, start the machine. No arguing, please."

Silently the girl sat down in the seat of the great contraption. Leaning forward she began adjusting the settings on some panel hidden from Hamilton's view. As she worked, Maxwell moved to the machine and sat beside her.

"It has been an honor, sir," he said. Hamilton did not reply, but watched sharply, his arms crossed over his chest.

"Here we go, then," said Florrie, pulling a large lever at her right hand. There was a great groaning of gears, and sparks began to spit from the metal box at the foot of the carriage. The hydraulic pistons began to move, gaining speed. Hot steam rose from the machine, and then all of a sudden the sparks became lighting, and the lightning became great arcing arms of power, and the tent was filled with a punishing blue-white radiance, blinding all three as the groan became a roar.

George Chrystal, twenty years old, stood in an empty office at the Cavendish Laboratory at Cambridge University, a sheaf of papers in his hand. Printed on the first page in large, neat letters was "Official Transcript, University of Aberdeen." In his other hand, Chrystal held his hat, doffed in anticipation of meeting the great James Clerk Maxwell, who was meant to be his new advisor.

But Maxwell could not be found, not by the secretary, not by the provost, and not by an anxiously wandering Chrystal, who had eventually returned to the great mathematician's empty office. Chrystal was well beyond boredom, and had moved into annoyance. Feeling frustrated and more than a touch disrespectful, he stepped behind Maxwell's desk and dropped into his chair.

Just at that moment there was a tremendous crashing noise from the next room, and a flash of blue light through the door window that dazed Chrystal for a moment. Convinced that he had somehow caused the concussion, Chrystal leapt from the chair and resumed his posture of waiting. This he held for only a moment before his attention wandered and he noticed the warm steam leaking from the edges of the door where he had seen the blue flash.

Chrystal didn't even bother struggling against his curiosity; he quickly pushed through the door and into the lab room next to the office. There he saw his new advisor, a sixteen-year-old girl, and a man dressed in the uniform of a Continental officer in the American Revolution.

"What day is it?" cried James Clerk Maxwell, leaping from the seat of an impossible machine.

"Oct—October 13th, 1871," replied Chrystal, beyond nonplussed. "About eight p.m., I think. I'm sorry I'm late; I missed the train."

"My dear Mr. Chrystal!" said Maxwell with a smile. "Of course. Then we're back in Cambridge. We were on a bit of a trip to the United States of Columbia, you see."

"The United States of Colombia?" asked Chrystal. "Where? Bogotá?"

"Virginia," said the man in the Revolutionary uniform.

"But that's in America," replied Chrystal dumbly. "And we're in England." He felt as though his mind simply wouldn't run, as though its gears were jammed. Was this what studying under Maxwell would always be like?

"Now then," said Maxwell. "Activate the cleaning machines if you please, Mr. Chrystal, and let's put tea on. I see you've come back, or forward, with us, Mr. President."

There was a pause of about fifteen seconds.

"Mr. Chrystal, the cleaning machines, please."

"I'm sorry," stammered Chrystal. "What machines?"

"He's new here, Max," piped up the young woman. "Poor thing, this must be his first day."

"Just my entry interview, actually," said Chrystal.

"Well, I'm Florence Douglas," said the girl, extending a hand. Chrystal took it, and promptly received an unexpectedly manly handshake.

There was a shout from the far end of the laboratory. "The cleaning machines! Where are they?" Maxwell was casting about frantically. "They took up the whole far wall— couldn't have been moved in an afternoon!" But the more he searched, the more Maxwell's panic seemed to grow. "My chemical batteries! My spring coasters! My clockwork butler!"

"What's the matter, Max?" said Miss Douglas, coming to the professor's side.

"Time is the matter, Florrie, dear," said Maxwell quietly. Walking back to where Chrystal and the officer stood near the great machine, Maxwell called out, "Mr. Chrystal! Where did you say the state of Virginia is?"

"America, sir, the east coast," replied Chrystal perplexedly. "Just next to Washington, D.C."

"That'll be District of Columbia," said Maxwell. He and Miss Douglas had reached the two young men. "It's all backwards, don't you see, Mr. President? Your refusal to lead the assault on redoubt ten has changed the whole course of history. The United States of America, the District of Columbia, Cambridge apparently being in— what did you call it, Mr. Chrystal, 'England?'— rather than Albion. And if the capital's in 'Washington'— perhaps I'm now wrong to call you Mr. President, Mr. Hamilton!"

"Surely these cosmetic changes are meaningless, Mr. Maxwell," said the officer called Hamilton. "America, Columbia— the nation is forged either way."

"No!" cried Miss Douglas. "It's far worse! Come see!" She had wandered to a large picture window, but now was running for the door to the street. She opened it and dashed out, the three men following close behind.

They spilled out onto Free School Lane, which bustled even at this hour with foot and carriage traffic moving through the heart of Cambridge. Miss Douglas had run to the end of the street, still frantically looking about for something.

"I don't understand," said Chrystal.

"I agree," said Hamilton.

"They're gone," moaned Maxwell. Looking out at the street, he saw gentlemen and laborers, ladies and their housemaids, carriages and coaches of all sorts. He saw a busker playing a violin on the corner. But mainly he saw what was lacking: the clockwork cleaners, the velocipedes, the self-altering shop signs, the clanking, coughing auto-carriages. The sky was woefully free of zeppelins or ornithopters of any sort.

Maxwell was pale. "It's gone, all of it. Everything that made the world wondrous."

Miss Douglas returned at a run. "It's the same everywhere," she said, shaking her head. "It's as though everything grand has been stripped from the world, and only the dull colors and unhappy people are left."

"Please, Mr. President, Mr. Hamilton," said Maxwell. "In some way your influence has been lost. You were a proponent of industrialization, were you not?"

"There was never a President Hamilton in America," said Chrystal suddenly. Viewing the shock and horror of Maxwell and Douglas had shaken something loose in his mind, and already he had worked out most of the facts, or what the facts must be, impossible as they seemed. The others turned to look at him. "Or I don't think so. Let's see: Washington, Adams, Jefferson—"

"Adams, that dog!" cried Hamilton. "Very well, Mr. Maxwell, tomorrow we shall end this terrible world of yours!"

"It's the only world we've got," said Chrystal, somewhat sadly.

The time carriage crashed to the earth from a height of about two feet. Everywhere was panic. Redcoats ran here and there, shouting as they took up firing positions behind a wooden parapet. Beyond the parapet Alexander Hamilton could see a ditch, and past that a thick criss-cross of wooden defenses. In the dark he made out what appeared to be Continental soldiers hacking at these outer fortifications. Then he realized with horror where he stood.

"We're on redoubt ten!" he cried to Maxwell and Florrie. "You've some aim, Mr. Maxwell!"

"Florrie, under the time carriage!" Maxwell shouted. Wordlessly the girl leapt from her seat to the ground, then shooting a spiteful look at Maxwell, reached back into the carriage and grabbed forth a rifle. She fell to one knee and began loading.

"Damned strong-headed girl," said Maxwell, accepting Hamilton's offered pistol. Hamilton himself drew his saber, a look of determination etched across his face.

"Who goes there?" cried a voice. The three turned to see an Albian officer looking out over the palisade, having apparently just spotted the Continental infantry chopping at the woodworks. It was the officer's last duty, however, for Hamilton acted swiftly to silence the man with his saber.

"Come on, boys! What took you so long?" Hamilton shouted from atop the palisade, where he had clambered as the Albian officer fell dying. The Continentals, looking up from their work, saw Hamilton silhouetted against the evening sky and gave a great cheer.

Hamilton leapt down from the palisade to see a handful of Albian infantry approaching him and his allies from the future. Florrie's rifle cracked, and the lead Albian fell with a shout. Maxwell, standing, carefully took aim with the pistol, fired, and missed.

"Too much time in the academy," he said as Hamilton reached his side. "I'm afraid I won't be much use here."

"Keep her safe," said Hamilton, nodding his head at Florrie.

"Yes, the poor girl," agreed Maxwell. "She's in terrible danger!"

"Danger, sir?" replied Hamilton. "She's our fire support!"

With the comforting bark of Florrie's deadly rifle in his ears, Hamilton ran for the cluster of Albian soldiers. He leapt at them wildly, stabbing one in the gut, then slashing another's throat before the stunned infantrymen could respond. Of the half-dozen who had come at him, four were now down. Liking these odds, Hamilton squared off against the other two.

"I'll weigh one Continental against two Albians any day, boys," he said tauntingly.

"That's as may be," laughed the man closing on his right hand, "but what about that lot?"

Hamilton turned to see another dozen or so Albians advancing at Florrie and Maxwell's rear.

"Mr. Maxwell!" he cried. "See to your charge!" He spun back around just in time to parry a low stab from the bayonet of the Albian who had spoken. Hamilton quickly turned his sword up and slashed the man across his chest; the wound was nothing fatal, but enough to force the man back a step or two while Hamilton turned his attention to the other fighter.

This fellow was apparently an officer, for he had a sword out as well. Hamilton feinted low, but the Albian wouldn't take the bait. They stood apart for a moment, judging each other, then the Albian looked to his left as he heard his companion coming back

up. Hamilton promptly lunged, putting his blade through the Albian's chest, where it stuck on a brass button as the man with the rifle approached.

The Albian raised his rifle preparatory for a vicious downward stab with the bayonet. Hamilton tugged desperately, but his blade wouldn't come free. He let go and leapt for his attacker, ducking low just as the bayonet came down, tearing a long, shallow gash along his back. He tumbled to the ground with the Albian in his grasp. They struggled for a moment, then Hamilton fell back, gasping, as he felt a sharp pain in his side.

Looking down, he saw a small boot knife sticking from his jacket. Furiously, he pulled it free, and felt a rush of pain and spilling blood from his side. He scrabbled up to his knees, then fell forward on the Albian soldier, burying the knife in his throat. Exhausted, Hamilton turned himself over to look back at Maxwell and Florrie.

Both were now struggling in the arms of Albian infantrymen. Hamilton cursed. Looking to his right, he saw the Continental soldiers struggling up the ditch below the palisade. They were coming, they were coming, just not fast enough.

"Rush on, boys!" called a high, female voice. "The fort's ours!"

The Albian holding Florrie clamped a hand over her mouth, but it was too late; the Continentals, having heard her cry and thinking the redoubt breached, began climbing onto one another's shoulders to make it out of the ditch. They broke over the palisade like a swarm of ants. And Alexander Hamilton, swiftly losing consciousness, saw amidst the glare and smoke of Albian grenades that the day, and his place in it, were well won.

"One might think we'd have all the time in the world," said Maxwell, "but unless we wish to spend the remainder of a year here, we'd best be off before we're too missed."

"I understand," said Hamilton, focusing more on the new medal on his chest than on his friend. He lay back in his hospital cot, and winced as the motion tugged on his wound.

"You know," he said, "you said I'd survive, but you might have mentioned I'd get a terrible mauling in the deal."

"Survive! Good god, man! I never said you'd survive!" Maxwell cried in surprise. "We saw just today that the future is a mutable thing. Did you really think— all your wild swordsmanship—"

Hamilton sat straight up. "You damned old fool! You said I'd be president, an act which requires me to live through the night!"

Maxwell just shook his head.

"I think we shall see that it's not so simple as all that," said Florrie, at the other side of Hamilton's bed. "For instance, did anyone else notice that Mr. Chrystal called Albion 'England?' Now why should a land that's had its old name for as long as anyone can recall get changed by something we did in 1781? It's already Albion, isn't it?"

"Indeed it is, Florrie, my dear clever girl," said Maxwell quietly. "Which suggests that at some point in the future, we shall return to some point even further in the past."

This is the story, in full, as my father told it to me. It is unaltered in all salient facts, and has been emended only where necessary to dramatize events my father glossed over. The names of the key players have been kept unaltered, although it remains to be seen whether some merciful editor will change or censor those.

Whether it is all true, or whether it was just the brain-fever of an aging old man, or a romantic yarn spun for his son, is for the reader to decide. As for myself, I know what I believe—but then I must admit that I have known where to find Mr. James Clerk Maxwell, first Cavendish Professor of Physics at Cambridge University, Albion, for many years; needless to say,

I have always been too afraid to visit him there.

Put to paper in the year of our Lord 1878 by your faithful recorder,
    James Alexander Hamilton

About the Author

Nathaniel Webb is an author, musician, game designer, and software developer. He lives in Portland, Maine with his wife, son, and double the recommended number of cats.

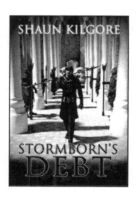

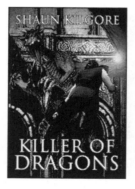
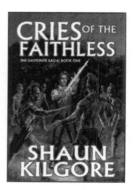

KEEPING UP APPEARANCES

BY KIT YONA

"Partner or cautionary tale?" she said, displaying a wide grin. The tip of her sword didn't waver. "Your choice."

Sparing the briefest of glances for the blade hovering near the rolls of fat that passed for his neck, the subject of her offer was silent for a moment, considering. In a voice laced with contempt he said, "You have no idea who you're dealing with, nor any idea the mistake you've just made." He tossed in a glare as well, but the dark-skinned woman's response was to show more teeth while snorting a laugh.

"Ah, don't sell yourself for a shaved copper, sir." She tapped his cheek with the flat of her blade, evoking a flinch. Brown eyes, dancing with either merriment or insanity, stayed locked with his. Around them the others in the gambling hall remained frozen in shocked silence, waiting to see how this was going to play out and calculating their options. "There's none here who don't know who you are." Her voice, redolent with the clipped endings and flat vowels that marked her as a Downsider, betrayed not a sign of nervousness. "Garandalen Dathenway, owner of this fine establishment and head of numerous other legally questionable business ventures in our fine city of Rockgate. One of the true powers here in Portside, as this little part of town is referred to by those who wouldn't venture down here on a bet. The rest of us just call you the Baron of Crumbletown." With graceful motions that spoke of extensive training she danced the point of her sword around the contours of his fleshy face, blood still just a promise for the time being. "I think I'm being quite reasonable about all this, don't you?"

Ignoring a bead of sweat that had begun to roll down the side of his face, The Baron sized her up with as much calm as he could muster. Tall and rangy, black hair in a braid over her shoulder. Unremarkable clothing. Held her weapon like she knew how to use it. "I think I'm the one being generous here, girl. After all, you aren't dead yet."

She tilted her head. "Is that so? And why such kindness, sir?"

His eyes flicked downward. "I just replaced the rugs, and wharfscum blood leaves intolerable stains."

Her face contorted in mock outrage. "Interesting time for insults, being on the wrong end of a sword and all. And such a hasty judgment, too. Think you know me, do you?"

"It's difficult to keep track of every filthy little weasel that crawls out of the canals and thinks higher of themselves than they ought to, but you've been quite busy nibbling away at my operations." The Baron steepled his fingers, a gesture designed to let his going-to-be-punished-later enforcers know it was almost time to act. "The Demon in the Darkness, Fire-Eyes, the Lady of Dark Shadows. Such evocative names!" He paused for a moment, chuckling. "'Lady,' indeed. You're just a guttersnipe with lofty aspirations."

"Who has a sword to your throat."

"Who has a sword to my throat," he agreed. "And who for some reason thinks I would be helpless in my own establishment." The Baron leaned forward a bit, stopping just before the keen edge could slice into his flesh. "You seem a comely lass. Stop this foolishness and I'll give you to my best brothel." He leaned back again. "It's not a bad life."

Her smirk spoke volumes, as did her blade rising to the level of his eyes. "Right, and I'm sure you know what it's like to be a whore."

The Baron's eyes narrowed. "Now it is you who presume to know me, trash."

Again, the barb failed to strike home. "I do know you. You're the person stalling on a decision. I don't have your qualms about ruining the carpet, so I'll ask but one more time—do we have a deal, or will you just add to my growing legend?" This time she offered no smile, mouth settling into a grim line.

The Baron knew the point of no return and shook his head with a heavy sigh. "All the way from Kessher, this rug. Such intricate design. Are you sure you won't just go outside and let me have you killed there? Those flagstones are well-acquainted with the blood of the foolish."

Her eyes rolled as she shook her head. "I don't think we're going to be able to work together. I keep asking for pertinent decisions and you keep offering threats." She gestured with her free hand. "Are you going to promise to cut off my finger if I say I don't like the drapes?" Her eyes flicked away for a second. "That's just an example. I actually like the drapes. They go well with this rug, so I can see why you wouldn't want to get blood—"

"Enough!" snapped the Baron. "When I get done with you the biggest piece left will be a finger." He looked to her right and gave a short nod, preparing to dodge and knock her blade away as Jepps, his chief enforcer, stepped forward and ran her through.

Jepps had indeed gotten himself close enough to make that strike, but as his face loomed over her shoulder it donned an apologetic smirk. "Sorry, Gar. Too good an offer to pass up."

The Baron's blood didn't actually run cold, but a chill rippled through his massive frame. "I'll double it."

His former employee shook his head. "It's not the coin. Gonna make me a partner, give me my own things to run." Jepps stepped up next to the woman, a large man brandishing a wickedly sharp blade that was too long to be a dagger but too short to be a sword. "The Lady here has some solid plans for knocking off the rest of bosses around here and having us take over the whole thing. No more stupid turf squabbles. Just us running everything from the Wall down." In a louder voice her said, "The Baron is stepping down and giving run of this place to me and the Lady of Dark Shadows! Anyone got a problem with that should say something now!"

The Baron looked elsewhere and found Tellep, a hulking brute of limited intelligence who had never forgotten the situation he'd been freed from. At the Baron's nod the behemoth pulled a cudgel from his belt and charged with a roar. Three steps in Tellep howled in pain as twin flashes of silver buried themselves in his legs, sending him crashing to the floor. A lean man with a short sword kicked away his club and dropped a knee on his back, pinning him in place. The Baron used the distraction to slip a knife from under his chair, which he kept pressed below the expanse of his torso.

"Anyone else?" Jepps said with an air of challenge, as if he'd taken Tellep down himself. When there were no takers he swung back to the Baron with an insolent grin in place. "Any others you wish to send to their deaths?"

"You and her," said the Baron in a whisper, shifting the grip on his weapon. "I'll cut the two of you up and mix the pieces together, then offer a prize for anyone who can solve the puzzle. Then I'll cook the remains into a stew and serve it to your families before killing them one by one, and -"

"No." With a fluid motion the one known as the Lady slid her blade back into her scabbard. "You will do nothing of the sort," she said in a throaty growl that the Baron felt as well as heard. "You were given an opportunity that you've chosen to

107

ignore. That was unwise."

The Baron prepared to strike as she leaned in, confident he'd be able to open her throat and end this farce. Yet as he tensed her eyes began to glow an angry, sullen red, while black smoke curled in thick plumes from her nose. Her jaw jutted out to accommodate the thick, jagged teeth that were sprouting, and she raised her hands to show fingers tipped with serrated claws the length of daggers. Terror numbed him as she reached out, his knife dropping from a nerveless grip and hitting the carpet with a silent thump.

Instead of striking her talons caressed the side of his face and neck, glinting edges causing no pain aside from the tiniest of jabs in one of his wattles of fat. Her eyes blazed even brighter than before as something gray and viscous hung from the corner of her mouth. All around them there was panic on numerous levels, the highest displayed by those in the immediate vicinity. Some were frozen with fear while other scrambled to get away, and prayers and curses in equal measure filled the air. A table overturned, sending mugs and money everywhere. One woman near the front entrance swooned as her eyes rolled back into her head, her slumping body caught by someone nearby. Jepps took a half-step away, blade at the ready.

And then, in a snap, her visage was back to what it been before. Within a few moments the place began to settle down, people questioning what they'd just seen. Not so for the Baron, who continued to gasp for breath while his face turned an alarming shade of scarlet. Spittle flecked his lips as his massive form quivered and spasmed, and he managed no final words before pitching forward as far as his body would allow.

"It seems that our business negotiations were a bit too spirited for him," said the Lady. "In any case, I welcome you to my newest gambling establishment and apologize for all the commotion. Please allow me to provide a drink on the house for everyone as a celebration of our new ownership!" She finished with a smile and a flourish before continuing in a lower volume. "Quesia. Janlo. Take the big one out back and see if he's open to a change in employers. If he is, patch him up. If not, well, you know what to do. Jarque and Lido. Haul the previous owner out front. There's a cart waiting. Make sure you pat him down first." She paused and gave the corpse a look. "All of him. Be thorough. Ronk, keep Glims and Marigold with you and sort out his crew here. Let those who want to walk walk and send the useless ones packing. Meet us back home later." She gave a head jerk at Jepps and said,

"C'mon, let's go talk." On her way out she pointed at the woman who'd fainted, still in the arms of her would-be rescuer. "Bring that one with us. She's got a pretty face and you know how this sort of stuff gets me all worked up."

They emerged to a dimly lit street, the fading alchemical mixture used to power the lampposts fighting a losing battle against the night. A two-wheeled cart sat nearby, the horse in the traces dozing. The Lady took a few steps away from the front door and motioned for Jepps to follow her.

"You don't need to worry about what just happened," he said as he donned a crooked grin. "I still stand with you."

She nodded. "That's fine, as long as you stand right there." At his puzzled expression she added, "Clear shot."

Whether or not he figured it out before the heavy crossbow bolt smashed through his skull didn't matter much, but the Lady leaned over before his body had even settled and said, "Sorry. You betrayed him and you'd betray me." Straightening up, she nodded at the man and woman who'd trotted over. "Nice shot, Zesti. Put him in the cart with the recently departed Baron and go to NorthWharf, dock twenty. Ship there called *Erlep's Folly*. First mate is Pretty Jengs—the name isn't accurate, but don't stare. She'll cut your nose to nuts." Handing them a small pouch, she said, "Tell her it's a shame our shipment is going to get lost at sea. Better give her the crossbow, too. Rumor has it Lord Rockgate has thrown open the coffers and hired a real sorceress to help him clean up this town, and I wouldn't want that traced back to us. Go."

A quick look around showed all was at it should be—bodies being hauled, crew bustling about, not a member of the Watch to be seen—so she headed off. After a few steps she was joined by Nibbles, who had the woman who had fainted inside on her feet, albeit swaying a bit. As their new gambling den fell out of sight behind them he passed her over to the Lady's offered arm and strode several paces ahead of them, eyes alert.

The fainter looked over at her new escort before tightening her grip and stifling a belch. "Ugh. Just a warning, Meski, I may still grace you with an artistic re-imagining of my dinner on the cobblestones." Brushing brown hair from her face, she held the back of her free hand against her mouth for a moment as they walked along. "I assume our portly friend met an unfortunate demise."

"Assume away," came the reply. "Given his girth and the stress of intense negotiations with the Lady of Dark Shadows, the Nightmare Reborn, the Demonness of the Downside, well, it's not surprising things ended the way they did."

"That last one is new." There was a pause, then a sigh. "Nobody suspected a thing, I imagine. Poison took him out quick?"

Meski waggled her free hand and tapped her thumb against a chunky ring on her heart finger. "Like always. Looked like he'd been frightened to death. My legend grows some more and his body'll be beneath the waves an hour after the ship clears the harbor tomorrow morning." She slid her arm around her companion's waist. "You do good work, Beya."

"Not that I ever get to see it for longer than a second or two."

"Well, quit passing out every time you do magic."

Beya scowled. "Find someone else to do your illusions, then."

Meski laughed and slid her arm around Beya's waist. "Not many around who can, darling. I think I'll stick with you, my delicate flower."

Beya muttered under her breath for a few seconds before saying, "Delicate flower my ass. Are you at least taking me home?"

"Of course! I know how you get after using magic."

"Nauseous?"

"No, *after* that." The twinkle in Meski's eyes indicated it was something she looked forward to as well.

"Oh, sure, blame it on me," Beya said in rough tones, failing to keep the corners of her mouth from curling up. "You could have just stuck your sword through his face."

"That sounds far too common a thing for a hellspawn such as myself to do," said the Lady of Dark Shadows as they turned onto Underhill Street. "Besides, did you see that carpet?"

About the Author

Kit Yona, in addition to working a less-than-glamorous day job, is a freelance editor and writer. Some of his previous works have appeared in Stupefying Stories, Femme Actuelle, and the #1bestselling Machine of Death anthology. He lives in New Jersey with his family and can be contacted at @theKitastrophe on Twitter.

Now Available
from all your favorite booksellers in
trade paper and electronic editions

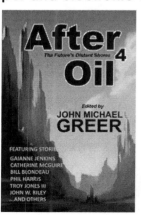

IN A GIANT'S EYE

BY SHAUN KILGORE

North of the Cumberlands, Walt and me saw our first giant tracks. We were hunting some of the big cats the city dwellers liked for their fancy shows when we spotted them. I never would have figured they would look so much like ordinary folks' feet only bigger. Goes to show how stories get all stretched out of shape.

Me and Walt trudged up a hill, mired in mud from the spring rains. At the top old Walt fell down into one of the footprints. I was laughing until I realized what it was.

"Would you look at that? I don't believe what I'm seeing."

Walt stood up in the center of the giant's footprint, trying to wipe away the mud. "What're you talking about, Loyd?"

Walt scrubbed his fingers on his coat and stepped out. He looked at the print then saw the next one. He pointed. "I don't believe it. Them's giant tracks, Loyd. My pa used to talk up stories about them giants. Always thought they was just talk."

"Looks like more than talk to me, Walt," I said.

"Yep, I reckon so, Loyd," said Walt.

I had this crazy thought. "You maybe want to follow them?"

Walt looked at me like I'd sprouted another head. "Follow them? Now why would we want to do a fool thing like that?"

"I don't know," I said. "Maybe we might get to see a giant for ourselves. It'd be something, Walt. That'd be a story to tell the boys around the shack."

"Humph. They'd believe anything. Their noses are already red before daybreak. I've never seen them with their senses about them."

"Come on. What could it hurt?"

Walt looked at me and sniffed. He hitched up his knapsack and snagged his bow from the ground where he'd dropped it. For a wonder, the arrows had stayed in his quiver. He gave me another look maybe to make sure I was serious.

"Alright. Let's go then," he said.

I smiled. "Off we go."

Following the trail of a giant wasn't a simple thing. No, you had to consider how tall they were and their gait. This giant must have been forty feet tall or better and moved easily over the uneven terrain of the mountainside. Me and Walt had a devil of a time keeping after the tracks. Trees, thick brush, and outcroppings of gray stone made the going rough. I was scaling the rocks and getting scratched up on brambles more often than following the footprints. Walt was cussing the whole way but he kept coming. Never once considered turning back. He was hooked on this crazy hunt as surely as I was. I just had to see one of them giants with my own eyes.

We spent the better part of the day on the trail, never once hearing a sound or catching a sign of the giant. The only constant was the footprints. Even when we did have to detour around some tree or rock, we still managed to pick up those tracks. They were a hard thing to miss. Our path continued deeper in to foothills. We encountered a few other animals but the woods seemed empty. My skin was crawling as we entered some early evening fog. We'd gone a let the day get away from us.

Darkness closed in on the mountains. Me and Walt finally had to stop and set up camp for the night. We hadn't had any luck at all. I was sure Walt was going to give me grief. Once we got our fire burning the crackle of the flames and the heat were soothing away the aches of the day's trek. Walt said nothing, which I took as a bad sign. I was just biding my time. He'd say something sooner or later. I knew Walt well enough by now. While I dreaded the words, Walt kept himself busy cooking some of the dried soup in a pan over the flames. Once he had it good and hot, with the smell of onions and garlic wafting in my direction, he spoke.

"You think we should keep following the trail?"

I sat up straight. I hadn't been expecting that question. I looked at Walt in the flickering firelight. His grizzled face just stared at me.

"I...I don't know, I guess. I mean, Walt, I thought you'd be giving me an earful and telling me what a waste of a good hunting day it's all been."

Walt scrubbed his day's growth of whiskers and pursed his lips for a second. "Well, I was aiming too, but I got to thinking about it, Loyd. I can't quite shake the idea. I think I need to see one of them giants for my own sake. I reckon the only way to do it is to keep after this one for as long as we can. And pray rain doesn't wipe the prints away."

"It'd be something, wouldn't it, Walt," I said softly.

"Sure would," Walt replied. He poured some of the soup into a tin cup, dug out a spoon from his sack, and handed it to me. "Eat up while it's hot. Shame I don't have some cornbread to go with it. That Millie Wite makes some fine cornbread. I'd like to pay her a visit once we get back."

I nodded and ate my soup and pondered the kinds of stories folk in the Cumberlands like to tell about giants. The old ones had the best stories, but also the ones that made you think they were winding them up just to get your eyes goggling out of your head. Of course, I wondered if maybe they were right. I looked around at the darkness that surrounded us in the mountain forests. Our little pool of light didn't offer much protection. Me and Walt were out with nothing but the trees and the stars overhead. The air was getting chilly so we both tried to hunker down as close as we could to the flames without catching ourselves afire. We had just a blanket apiece. We'd had the sense to wear thick wool coats and pants along with long-uns that we wore underneath them. I brushed my fingers against the bow and the arrows. Then I made sure I had my knife loose nearby just in case. Satisfied, I tucked my cap down low near my eyes so my ears were covered and tried to sleep.

Of course, I couldn't sleep at all. How could I? That giant could be lurking out there in the dark just waiting for us to doze off. Maybe it knew we'd been following it? Now it was just getting ready to pounce on us like one of the big cats. My eyes came open. I'd turned my head away from the campfire so I wouldn't be blinded. The only thing I could see was darkness and the outlines of fir trees and few of the rocks that seemed to grown right out the grass. The little clearing we'd chosen was a flat shelf surrounded by steeper hills. We were about a hundred paces east of the tracks.

The woods were completely still. The fire had died down a bit. Occasionally, I could hear Walt's soft snores behind me. Seems he didn't have a lick of trouble bedding down. I yawned and rubbed my eyes. I was being a fool. Letting the excitement carry me away. I was giving that giant too much credit maybe. Yep, that was it. Next I'd be jumping at shadows. I shook my head and closed my eyes again.

A branch snapped somewhere above us.

I jerked up, knife gripped tightly in my hand. I was wide-eyed and my heart was hammering my chest. I was short of breath so I couldn't get Walt's attention. *He was still sleeping!* I stared up to where I thought the sound had come from, just waiting maybe for something to happen. There wasn't another sound. That didn't matter much though. I wasn't going to sleep a wink now.

While I did catch a few snatches of sleep, I spent that night staring into the darkness just listening and maybe waiting. Walt continued snoring away. The fire died down a bit so I tossed more wood on it to keep it bright so I could see as much as possible. My eyes were burning come morning. Walt opened his eyes and stretched wide, even yawning again. He scrubbed his beard and looked over at me. I was staring into the flames.

"What's wrong with you? Didn't you sleep?"

I shook my head. "Nope. I thought I heard something."

Walt shook his head and set about cooking a bit of breakfast for the both of us. He did most of the cooking seeing as I was just plain awful at it. I got up to stretch my legs. I was yawning something fierce and trying to clear my eyes. The sun was just barely up and the forest was still dim. I walked around the clearing looking at dull gray stone and wandered among the closest brush to see if I could find the branch. I climbed a slight hill that wound up around the rocks. Looking back down, I had a clear view of our camp below.

I listened but the birds and other critters were making their usual amount of noise for daybreak. I let my eyes rove around slowly, trusting my hunter's instincts to spot some sign, no matter how small. The smells coming from the cook fire were distracting me some. My stomach rumbled. I went back the edge and looked down. Walt was whistling softly and adding some spice or other to the pot.

I saw the branch. Then I saw a footprint. A new one.

"Walt!"

"What is it, Loyd?"

"You've got to see this."

Walt muttered to himself but left the fire and scaled the hill path and met me at the top. I pointed to the fresh track.

"See. I knew I heard something."

Walt examined the footprint. It was shallower than the ones we'd been following.

"Looks like he was trying to be sneaky," said Walt.

I turned around and squinted in the half-light, moving away from Walt, I looked for the same lighter depressions in the grass. *There! And there!*

"Walt, I found some more of these new tracks."

Walt stood up and joined me as we hunched around a few of the giant's footprints. Walt frowned after a few minutes. He touched the ground in the middle of the prints. "Loyd, there's something odd about these. Other than them being not so deep."

"What?" I asked.

"I think they're smaller than the others too," said Walt.

"Smaller? What do you mean?"

"I mean they're not the same tracks at all. I think there might be two of them giants roaming in these mountains."

I glanced around at the trees and then up and down the slope. There was nothing in the woods but Walt and me as far as I could tell. How could something so big hide so easily? It didn't seem possible. My skin crawled. *The giant could be watching us right now*, I thought.

Walt sniffed. "Come on. Let's go eat." He turned and headed back down to the camp.

I watched him climb down, but couldn't get my feet to move. I was rooted there like a tree just listening and maybe hoping I'd catch the giant taking a peek. I was being a damned fool maybe. A monster that big that could be quiet enough to come up to the edge of our camp in the darkness wouldn't be so easy to catch. I kicked the ground and trudged downhill, eased down the path so I wound around the rocks without much trouble and came up the campfire. Walt was serving up something in the bowls.

I couldn't be sure what. It was spiced up with pepper though; I could smell it. "What's this?"

"Breakfast," said Walt. He was smiling.

I rolled my eyes. "I know it's breakfast. But what is it?"

I peered into the bowl. It was white and grainy.

"Grits," Walt answered. "Hominy grits. Fresh ground 'fore we left."

I nodded appreciatively and spooned some into my mouth. I gagged at the pepper. "Gaa. Too much blasted pepper, Walt. How do you taste anything anymore?"

Walt ate his grits contentedly. "I don't know what you mean. The black pepper just brings out the flavors, you know."

Not wanting to waste it, I scooped up the rest of the grits and swallowed half the water from my canteen. My tongue was burning.

We started breaking out camp. As I rolled up my blanket, I looked at Walt who was kicking dirt on the fire. "You think we should keep following the first set of tracks?"

Walt scrubbed his hands on his coat and shoved the pot back into his knapsack. He nodded. "I do. We'd be fools to try and track the others. Not sure we'd be able to keep on the trail. I'd rather trust the tracks I can see better."

I wasn't sure why but I wanted to follow the second set. I didn't say anything though since Walt was probably right. I just grabbed my quiver and bow and headed back to the first sets of footprints. Me and Walt took off after the trail like a couple of hounds trying to root out a rabbit. With a whole day ahead of us, we were bound and determined to catch our glimpse of one of them giants.

After hiking uphill for a while, I started thinking about this hunt we were on. Me and Walt weren't aiming to kill one, since neither of us knew whether our arrows would do the job. So if we weren't going to kill a giant, what were we going to do? Wouldn't it be good to have proof we'd seen one? Of course, what kind of proof could we get? I was tumbling those kinds of thoughts around in my head while my legs were beginning to ache from the climbing. Walt, for a wonder, wasn't cussing. Also might have been because he was concentrating on breathing and climbing like me. The air seemed to change too. Not sure what I mean but it got harder to breath the higher we went up.

I'd never strayed so far from our usual hunting trails. We'd been seeing lots more critters skulking nearby like they was curious about us. Not sure many people ventured so high in the mountains anyway. Sort of made sense that the giants lived up here though. Not many men would find travel through tangled forests all that easy.

That was another thing. As we continued following the trail, the signs of the giant's path became much clearer too like it wasn't trying to conceal itself. Broken limbs and shrubs torn clean out of the ground. Even some of the smaller rocks were rolled out of the way so the giant wouldn't have to go around. Me and Walt had to find ways around a few of the holes left from where the rocks used to be just so we could return to the trail. It was exhausting work, made more so by our haste to find something, anything. We were so focused on the search for the first giant that all thought of the second one faded from our minds.

Hours passed. We stumbled onto a creek that cut through a series of ravines. We stopped to refill our canteens and take a rest. Lunch was some crumbly bread and chunks of dried venison. Wasn't the tastiest meal, but it served well enough. We were both used to living almost hardscrabble off the land. We'd ranged widely as hunters and trackers for all manner of reasons--though most of them came down to filling our bellies and putting a few coins in our pockets. This was probably our greatest hunt yet, but it would go down as just a story.

"What if we could trap the giant," I said.

Walt gave me a dumbfounded look over his shoulder. He was a few paces above me sitting on a flat rock, resting against the trunk of a gnarled tree.

"You out of your head, Loyd? How the hell we supposed to trap a giant? We don't have the gear and who knows if we could rig up something strong enough to trap it. Then what do we do if we did get one? How would we be getting it down from the mountain? Sheesh, boy, have some sense, would you. Ain't gallivanting up here to see them good enough?"

I didn't want to say no. He'd given me an earful; that was enough. I probably deserved it too. I thought it through and couldn't come up with much else to say so I just kept quiet and rested for a bit more. Walt called an end to our little lunch break and we were headed out again. The trail was getting harder to follow. The ground was getting steeper, the path rockier, and the tracks themselves were harder to make out. Still, me and Walt kept going.

Sometime after midday, I was stopped short by the sound of these awful moans. Walt went stiff, stopped just ahead of me, and drew an arrow. He nocked his bow and spun around slowly. He exchanged a look with me.

I readied my bow too. The moaning echoed off the rocks and seemed to carry over the mountain.

Birds burst out of a stand of willow trees. Walt cursed but held the arrow.

"Can you tell where it's coming from?"

Walt shook his head. "Not with all these rocks around us. The sound bounces around funny."

I closed my eyes for a minute and tried to sort out the noises. I turned round and round slowly. The moans made me shiver. What was making them? Was it the giant? Or some other hurting creature? The echoes rebounded on another and mixed together.

"Let's keep to the path," said Walt.

I opened my eyes. He was facing me though his eyes were roving everywhere like he expected something bad to happen.

"Okay," I said.

I followed behind Walt, keeping much closer to him than I had been. I didn't want to get separated. We traveled along, eyes trained on the ground for the giant's footprints as often as they were looking to the trees, the rocks, and the other underbrush. We climbed up the slope as it rose up again. The moaning followed us until we crested the top and stood on a ridge. Thereafter, it stopped and a deep quiet dropped on the forest.

Walt held up a hand when he looked down the opposite side. I was a few paces behind him, sweating and mumbling about my sore toes. I nearly ran into his palm.

"What is it, Walt?"

"Giants," he said softly.

I gulped. "What do you mean?"

Walt knelt down so he was concealed by some tall weeds. The trees were spaced thin and two tall oaks rose up on either side and formed a natural gateway.

He motioned me to get on my knees. I did and then crawled up beside him. Down at the bottom of a ridge mostly free of trees, we saw not just one giant but what had to be twenty of them. They were gathered around tiny fires that barely smoked let alone offered much warmth.

"What do we do, Walt?"

"Hell if I know," he said softly. "Sure wasn't expecting a tribe of them."

A twig snapped nearby. I jerked my head towards the sound. My eyes took in the sight in stages, head then moving up and up until I reached the top or the head of a gigantic woman standing not more than a few paces behind us.

"Walt," I struggled to say.

He turned back then gasped. "Well, would you look at that?"

I was looking but not really believing what I was seeing. The woman towered over us. She was dark of hair and wrapped in animals skins--large ones. *Probably a bear*, I thought absently. Her skin was weathered from living outdoors. She watched us with her fierce green eyes. I felt my heart pounding my chest. No one moved. She took a step forward and felt the earth tremble ever so slightly. Her bare foot, almost as big as my chest, left the same soft impression in the ground.

"You were the one watching our camp." I clamped my teeth shut with a loud click. I hadn't meant to speak.

The giant frowned at me and narrowed her eyes. She didn't seem to understand.

The moans started up again but from our position at the top of the ridge, we realized the sound was coming from the giant encampment below us. Walt turned his attention away slowly.

"Neva!"

The giant's words were firm. Her eyes smoldered and she shook her head. Walt froze. He held up his hand and nodded at the giant. He looked at me but didn't move a muscle or say anything.

"What does that mean?" I asked.

"Neva," the giant repeated. The words were lower and reminded me of thunder.

The moans died down again and we could make out the faint noises of the giants all seeming to talk at once. The woman took another step. She sniffed then rubbed her nose in agitation. She seemed hesitant.

Maybe we smell bad.

I smiled. It had been a few days since I'd bathed. I probably smelled something awful. The giant noticed my smile and her frowned deepened.

"Tuka ra el." The giant gestured with her arms, urging us to stand up. I reached for my bow but she pointed at me. "Neva a culu." The giant came closer so that we had to look almost straight up to see her face. She gestured again. We obeyed.

Me and Walt were being led down into the camp of giants. The climb down was tough, the ground uneven, filled clumps of weeds and loose stone in equal measures. I slipped a couple of times. The giant went last and I was worried she'd cause the whole side of the ridge to slide. Walt was having a devil of time keeping his footing. I was more surefooted than he but still the going was slow.

"Tuka ra el," the giant repeated.

"I'm going," I said softly.

The giant grunted. Her shadow fell over us so that it seemed like twilight for the last several paces. Not far from the bottom, the first of the giants in the camp spotted us. The news spread quickly so that when we were down on flatter ground, there was a chorus of rumbling giant voices filling the air. Some of them didn't sound all that hospitable. I was thinking they seemed downright angry. Maybe they had reason to be. After all, we were trespassing, I reckon. That also meant we were in a heap of trouble.

The giant woman ushered us into the camp and the crowd of giants who were staring down at us like we were bugs they were meaning to crush soon surrounded us. There was only one other woman as far as I could tell. The majority of the giants were bigger and bulkier men wearing the same patchwork skins as the woman was, but which left the stone-like chests bare. One of the giants was wearing crown of sorts made from metal or wood; I couldn't be that sure. He suddenly knelt down to look at us, sniffing the air the same way the woman had. He winced.

"Takina," he rumbled. He looked at the others who were circling us. "Takina fulu." There were murmurs but the sounds were so deep I could barely make out the words.

"What do we do?" I whispered.

Walt grimaced. "Get ready to be somebody's dinner, I bet."

The giant came closer so I could see his stony face with its wiry beard. His eyes were blue and glistening. He looked directly at me.

"You are far from home, manling."

My eyes went wide. So did Walt's.

"You speak with our words."

"Mmm," he rumbled. "I know your tongue, manling. Why are you here?"

"I...that is, we were following the footprints of one of...of your people. We're hunters and trackers by trade."

"It has been many years since a manling has been seen in these places. But, you lie, do you not? Was it not you who struck Makura?" The giant's voice was more like a growl now. He was clearly agitated.

"Who? We ain't hurt nobody," said Walt. "Like Loyd said we just found some tracks and thought it be something to see one of you giants. I just thought you were stories my pap told me."

I thought for a moment. "Is this Makura the one making all the noises?"

"Yes. Makura is young and ventured down the mountain too far and was attacked by manlings. He was hit in the eye with one of your weapons. Do you deny that you were the one who harmed him?"

"Yes, we do," I said. Walt, standing next to me, nodded vigorously. "Can we do anything to help?"

The giant considered this. He consulted the circle of giants and there were more deep rumbles like we were in the center of a big storm. When he looked down at us he clenched his jaw.

"Come with me."

We followed the giant and were followed by the others. The earth seemed to heave beneath our feet so that Walt and me stumbled and wobbled more than we actually walked to where the one called Makura lay sprawled out on furs near one of the fires.

I saw the fletching from the arrow before I realized it was protruding from the giant's eye. It seemed so small lodged there in one corner just under the eyelid. Makura was grunting and heaving something fierce. As we neared him, he let loose more of the moans we'd been hearing. The sound was so loud we had to cover our ears. Once they'd subsided turned to the giant wearing the crown.

"Why don't you remove the arrow?"

The giant held up hands bigger around than my entire head. The fingers were as thick as my arms. "Too small, manling. We cannot dislodge it without damaging Makura's eye."

Walt looked at me and tried to shake his head slowly while he mouthed the word 'no.'

"I'd like to help get that arrow out, if I could." I said it but then couldn't believe I'd said it at all. I was being a fool again. Of course, it didn't matter much since we were probably going to die anyways.

The 'king' or whatever he was conferred again with those who hand followed us. The giant's speech was strange. There were soft denials and harsh condemnation in the way they moved though. Finally the king looked at us again.

"Do what you can, manling."

My mouth was so dry but I didn't dare reach for my canteen. The two of us ventured closer to Makura so that we were standing right next to his enormous head. I was able to get a better look since the giants stayed where they were. I was grateful for the space myself. Walt seemed to breathe easier too.

The shaft of the arrow was buried almost half way in, but it wasn't truly in the eyeball itself. The head had grazed it, that was true, but the arrow was pinned in the tender flesh of the eyelid and the skin that surrounded it.

"You think you can get that damned thing out, Loyd?" Walt was peering up at Makura. The woman giant had returned and knelt down on the opposite side of the injured one.

"Maybe," I said.

I came even closer. Makura turned up his nose. "Takina fulu," he bellowed. The giant had smelled us now, but couldn't see through the watery eye.

The woman giant pressed a hand onto Makura's chest and spoke in what sounded like a soothing tone. I needed to get to work. I'd skinned game often enough so I knew how to use a blade for such things. I even tinkered a bit with doctoring when me or Walt got cuts or scrapes.

I moved up the head and grabbed the shaft of the arrow and moved it ever so slightly. Makura winced but did not cry out, or move much at all. I choked back my own cry and took a shuddering breath. I worked carefully so I wouldn't tear the skin too much. The head of the arrow came loose from one place.

"Gah!" Makura bellowed.

I jumped back and waited.

The woman was stroking Makura's chest and whispering again.

I approached again but was breathing deeply through my nose while biting my lip. I worked with the shaft until it pulled free from the skin behind the eyelid. Rivulets of blood streaked down the cheek. I kept going since I was able to get my fingers on the arrow's head I pressed until it snapped. The barbed metal came away in my hand. I tossed it to Walt who was perched almost on my shoulder watching the whole thing.

With the head out of the way, I slipped the shaft through the pierced eyelid and finally pulled it free completely. Makura let out a deep sigh of relief. So did I.

Me and Walt left the camp of giants unharmed. The king, Eran, thanked us for helping Makura and rewarded us with a few ornate rings that were giant-made so that they were more like crowns than something you'd fit on your finger. We descended the mountain and returned to the Cumberlands three days after we left our usual hunting trails. We told our stories to a lot of the local folks. Most didn't believe us until we pulled out the jeweled rings. Me and Walt had one heck of a time let me tell you.

About the Author

Shaun Kilgore is the author of various works of fantasy, science fiction, and a number of nonfiction works. He has also published numerous short stories and collection. His books appear in both print and ebook editions. Shaun is the publisher and editor of MYTHIC: A Quarterly Science Fiction & Fantasy Magazine. He lives in eastern Illinois. Visit www.shaunkilgore.com for more information.

Don't Miss an Issue!

Subscribe to MYTHIC: A Quarterly Science Fiction & Fantasy Magazine

U.S. Subscribers
4 Issues... $40.00

International Subscribers
Inquire on rates at by email at info@mythicmag.com

For full subscription information go to:

www.mythicmag.com

REVIEWS

"FEDERATIONS" AND "THE BEST AMERICAN SCIENCE FICTION AND FANTASY 2016" EDITED BY JOHN JOSEPH ADAMS

REVIEWED BY STEPHEN REID CASE

Federations
John Joseph Adams, editor

Every anthology is, by definition, a mixed bag. That's the point. But there are different kinds of bags, and the pair of anthologies under review, while both under the editorial direction of the prolific John Joseph Adams, provides examples of two very different types of collections. The first is a theme anthology in which each story was selected for a specific trait. The second is a showcase anthology, representing the best speculative fiction of the past year. We'll start with the theme anthology.

Science fiction tells some of the largest stories possible. Where else do you have narratives that span not just continents and lifetimes but rather planetary systems and millennia, or where can you find stories of empires that span galaxies and warfare that lasts beyond the lifetime of a single species? Science fiction imagines what happens when you take political structures, culture, or military conflict and expand these to the largest spatial and temporal scales possible. Of course not all science fiction plays to these scales, but this magnitude of scope is part of what makes greats like Ender's saga, the *Dune* chronicles, or Asimov's *Foundation* work.

But Ender's saga, *Dune*, and *Foundation* are multi-volume epics. Is it possible to take the largest scale and scope of science fiction and capture it instead in a short story? This would be quite the trick, as short stories are by definition the opposite of long and epic. John Joseph Adams tackles the challenge of collecting stories that attempt just this in *Federations*, an anthology original published in 2009 but recently reissued.

This juxtaposition of immense scale with concise narrative is on the one hand quite difficult yet on the other a hallmark of much of classical science fiction. This may explain Adam's tact in the anthology of mixing pieces by well-known authors with stories original to the collection. The result works well: an anthology of engaging short stories, each told against independent and immense vistas of interstellar war, culture, commerce, and politics—in other words, galactic federations.

Some of the reprints in this collection are of exceptional quality. Alastair Reynold's "Spirey and the Queen," for instance, is a prime example of the aim of the collection: a mystery and tight plot involving a single, compelling character played out against a carefully crafted background that includes planetary evolution, developing AI, and the fate of humanity itself. Another excellent reprint is Robert Silverberg's terrifying "Symbiont," in which the horror of galactic war plays into the encounter between the human nervous system and a terrifying form of alien life.

The original pieces though are what in my opinion make this anthology shine. "Carthago Delenda Est," for example, by Genevieve Valentine, tells the story of patient interspecies diplomacy against a background of possible galactic enlightenment, while "Twilight of the Gods," by John C. Wright, takes the epic scope of science fiction and plays it through the lens of fantasy, creating a medieval society living inside generational starships and offering a view of what galactic warfare might looks like through their eyes. "My She" by Mary Rosenblum, creates a starfaring culture and unveils it slowly to the reader through the eyes of the characters unlikely and surprising. Rosenblum does not only create this world though—in a matter of pages she has opened the door for its radical transformation.

Some of the stories take the tropes of epic science fiction and turn them on their head for comedic effect. "Terra-Exulta," by S. L. Gilbow, for instance, offers a wonderful tongue-in-cheek look at the arrogance of ecological engineering on planetary scales, and "The One with the Interstellar Group Consciousness," by James Alan Gardner, takes the concept of a self-conscious galactic civilization bored with its own existence and looking for that perfect someone/society/consciousness to merge with. It's like Seldon's psychohistory or *Star Trek*'s Borg collective meets *Seinfeld*.

Two pieces in this collection stood out for their style and tone. "The Cultural Archivist," by Jeremiah Tolbert, looked at the sinister side of an exploration regime (complete with Red Shirts), examining cultural exploitation in a story with a snappy rogue hero, lots of panache, and fantastic new technology tossed out like firecrackers throughout the work. The volume concluded with the incredibly beautiful "Golubash, or Wine-Blood-War-Elegy," by Catherynne M. Valente, that encapsulated fascinating xenobiology, interplanetary commerce, and the history of war, all told through the lens of a series of wine-tastings.

The common thread throughout these stories, besides the scale with which they grappled, is familiar to readers of science fiction: a clear sense of wonder. They explored ideas of what humanity and human endeavors might become on the very broadest scales, on the biggest maps possible, but they remained grounded in the narrative of individuals, the fabric of short stories themselves.

This is a remarkable accomplishment, and it says something about an enduring goal of science fiction: not simply to present new horizons or examine new technologies, but to imagine the human experience against these bright galactic backdrops.

The Best American Science Fiction and Fantasy
Karen Joy Fowler, Editor
John Joseph Adams, Series Editor

This next anthology does not have a specific focus but rather an immense mandate, one that both the series editor and the volume editor set up in their respective introductions. The goal is to showcase the very best works in speculative fiction appearing this past year (2015). This means that rather than exploring work of a specific tone or style, this anthology is helpful for getting a sense of the current state of speculative fiction. What is science fiction and fantasy saying right now? Where is the best fiction being published? Where is the boundary or the overlap between fantasy and science fiction?

Let me take the first question last. As I was reading these stories, it occurred to me that the difference between scifi and fantasy might be one of orientation, of the direction in which the authors are asking questions. Science fiction is a means by which writers peer out toward the horizons, probing the edges of the current human experience and pushing contemporary technologies or conditions toward possible future outcomes. By doing this, the best science fiction holds up a mirror to understanding ourselves in the here and now.

Take for instance Seth Dickenson's "Three Bodies at Mitanni," which is one of what might be considered the most straightforward science fiction pieces in the anthology. Within a story about a future Earth utopia exploring possible evolutions of humanity, Dickenson gives a deep and philosophically grounded discussion of human consciousness itself, as well as the nature of betrayal and forgiveness. Or take Catherynne M. Valente's "Planet Lion," which against a background of interstellar war looks at the imposition of military structure (and the uniformity it entails) on a planet of apex carnivores bound together in a planet-wide shared consciousness. These stories take big science fiction ideas but use them to examine what colonialism or survival might truly cost.

Fantasy, on the other hand, is when authors do the same thing but in the opposite direction. Instead of peering outward toward the borders of technological possibility or future conditions, they look inward to shine a light in the crevices and myths of the human experience and the wonder and mystery this has always entailed. Thus you have pieces like Will Kaufman's "Things You Can Buy for a Penny," about family, choices, and freedom, but most of all about bargaining with fate. The fact that it has a magic wishing well and a creature living within it doesn't make it any less true but somehow makes it truer. It is fantasy's acceptance of things that are not objectively true but somehow *should be true* that gives it its power, most illustrated here in Vandana Singh's "Ambiguity Machines: An Examination," a gorgeous Borgesian odyssey that uses ancient technologies to push and prod at the longings of the human heart. The machines are certainly fantasy, but, like Borges's labyrinths, a casual acceptance of the unreal or impossible is what makes the story so effective.

What about the second question, where is great science fiction and fantasy being published right now? This volume shows that *Uncanny Magazine*, a relative newcomer, has been firmly established alongside standbys like *Lightspeed, Asimov's, The Magazine of Fantasy and Science Fiction, Clarkesworld,* and *Strange Horizons*, which all have work in the collection. *Terraform*, the online publication by Motherboard, also has a piece represented. There are also stories from more mainstream literary markets, including *Harper's* and *The New Yorker*—though purists may quibble that while excellent pieces of literature (in particular, Adam Johnson's "Interesting Facts" is an exemplary work dealing with cancer and motherhood from a point of view continuing after death) they have such slender margins of the fantastic as to question their inclusion.

Finally, my first question: what is speculative fiction saying right now? In this anthology, the answer seems to be that the best science fiction and fantasy right now are stories tackling loss. There is certainly wonder here and no question that these are stories of the highest caliber, but they carry a deep sadness throughout. A good example of this is Kij Johnson's "The Apartment Dweller's Bestiary," which

in a sequence of short, disassociated vignettes explores the imaginary beasts that live quiet lives alongside modern humans. The domestic unreality of these creatures though provides a lens by Johnson magnifies the isolation and loneliness of modern apartment-dwelling humans.

I have already mentioned Valente's "Planet Lion," which expands the loss of war to costing the mind and identity not only of individual soldiers but of an entire planet. Liz Ziemska's "The Mushroom Queen" uses the fascinating and horrifying science of mushrooms to look at another kind of domestic absence, while "Rat-Catcher's Yellow," by Charlie Jane Anders, and "Interesting Facts," by Adam Johnson, both deal in beautiful and nuanced ways with loss caused by illness. Nick Wolven pushes the concept of loss further in "No Placeholder for You, My Love," imagining loss in a virtual world created for the eternal futility of searching for true love, and the narrative of loss reaches its climax with Maria Dahvana Headley's "The Thirteen Mercies," a mind-bending and heartbreaking look at the ultimate costs of war.

I don't think the editors meant to create a depressing work. But I wonder what it means that so many authors are creating such beautiful work about isolation, emptiness, departure, and loss. This is not to say there's a total lack of optimism, either in the collection itself or in any work taken alone. "By Degrees and Dilatory Time," by S. L. Huang, for instance, is about the loss of vision from cancer and yet in its honest treatment and portrayal (by an author who is herself a two-time cancer survivor) becomes one of the most hopeful pieces of the collection. Likewise the pieces by Singh and Dickenson and even the concluding short piece by Ted Chiang, "The Great Silence," which examines extinction and communication, capture bits of the optimistic wonder that was once standard (and a sometimes deadening effect) in science fiction and fantasy.

I don't point out this tone to say that speculative fiction has lost something or that it is a bad thing that some of the best stories right now seem to be some of the saddest. It's simply that a sense of loss is a very real and heavy thing that runs through this year's collection. If that resonates with you (and I feel this year that tone might indeed resonate with many of us) and you want a sense of what 2015 held for fiction and care about the state of the field, this anthology is required reading. If you want less of a focus on the most current fiction though and prefer science fiction from the past couple decades focused on the grandest scope and scale of the genre, then pick up *Federations* as well. Because both of these works show that the genre still has endless room for stories.

REVIEW
"DARK PEAK" BY
GEORGE R. FEHLING

REVIEWED BY FRANK KAMINSKI

**George R. Fehling's *DARK PEAK*
(Founders House Publishing,
October 2015, 259 pages, $15.99)**

George R. Fehling's novel *Dark Peak* is both an effective thriller and a heartfelt eco-polemic. Set in rural Vermont a century from now, it portrays a community at war over the fate of the rich forest ecosystem that surrounds it. Oil has long since depleted to the point of being nonviable as an energy source, and technolo-gies that once ran on oil—to the very limited extent that these still exist—now must be powered by biofuels. Up to this point, the community has produced its biofuels sustainably; but now rapacious outsiders have muscled their way into the local biorefining operation, intent on liquidating the forests in a futile bid to bring back the affluence of the industrial era. It's a revealing conflict, and one that Fehling feels certain will play itself out in the future in many places where dense forestland is to be found.

The community described above is Pleasant Valley, and it's northern Vermont's largest producer of canola, soy and sunflower seeds. A company named Pleasant Valley Biofuels converts these seeds into liquid fuels for lighting, heating, transport and running heavy machinery. There are, however, no working automobiles in Pleasant Valley, and only a precious few airplanes. This is because the entire community lies within the estate of the biofuels company's chief executive, Kenan Wales, and Wales has a strict conservation ethic. He remembers well the lessons of a recent historical interval known as "the Troubles," when industrial civilization collapsed as a result of outstripping its resource base. Thus, he's determined to see to it that production and consumption of liquid fuels within the region don't exceed what can sustainably be produced. In his view, biofuels shouldn't be wasted on joy riding, but should instead be reserved for critical uses like mail delivery, agriculture, commerce and medicine.

The majority of Pleasant Valley's inhabitants get around by foot or on horseback, and live without most of the modern-day comforts we take for granted. Like serfs on a medieval manor, they predominantly earn their livelihoods by tending the vast fields of oilseed crops around the Wales family mansion, or by working as servants for the Wales. Others are employed by a local military force known as the Northern Vermont Militia, which is led by the shady, opportunistic Captain Christopher Peck.

There's also an underground rebel movement whose aim is to put Pleasant Valley Biofuels out of business before it can usher in a repeat of the ruin that attended humankind's love affair with oil. With their unending campaign of sabotage attempts, these rebels have proven such a menace to the Wales family and the militia that a castle-like wall has been built to keep them at bay. The rebels live in subterranean hovels and fight with bows and arrows, but they nonetheless manage to inflict serious losses on their foes through their superior stealth and resourcefulness. My favorite trick of theirs involves using an old abandoned ski lift as a zip-line to quickly get from one place to another under the cover of night.

As for the villainous out-of-towners, they represent the leadership of a company called American Agrifuels. They've traveled all the way to Pleasant Valley from Albany, New York (hence their nickname, "the Yorkers"), ostensibly to celebrate their forthcoming merger with Pleasant Valley Biofuels. Yet all is not as it seems with these folks.

Our main hero is Amariah Wales, the son of the noble family. At just 19, he's a brilliant chemist and the brains behind the R&D division of his family's company, having made major breakthroughs in improving the energy density and winter performance of aviation fuel. It's a foregone conclusion that he will one day lead the entire enterprise. Yet he's unhappy. As good as he is at his job, he really doesn't fit into the company culture, much less into the aristocratic social circle to which his parents belong. He finds it much easier to relate to the servants who prepare his meals and clean up after him. And he's unmoved by the prospects of becoming the heir to Pleasant Valley Biofuels or wedding any of the well-to-do young ladies his parents keep sending his way, since either of these would put the kibosh on his dreams of traveling and seeing the world.

Thus, Amariah is less than pleased to learn that his parents intend for him to take over the company much sooner than he'd previously thought, which is to say immediately. His mother drops this news on him as the two prepare for a banquet they're hosting for the visiting American Agrifuels execs. She says Kenan plans to announce at the banquet that Amariah will be chief executive going forward. Amariah is crestfallen at this but resigns himself to his parents' decision. Little does he suspect the tragic turn to come, which will transform him into so much more than just the new company head.

For the sake of not giving away spoilers, I won't go into too much detail about the above-mentioned tragedy, except to say that it occurs when the Yorkers double-cross their new business partners to seize control of operations at Pleasant Valley Biofuels. Bent on returning as much of the northeastern United States as they can to an industrial-era standard of living, the Yorkers plan to dramatically ramp up the company's output using a brand-new process for converting trees into cellulosic ethanol. The only problem is that they require Amariah's expertise to do this, and Amariah is now missing in action. The rebels, knowing that the fate of the forests hangs in the balance, have whisked him away to a safe house.

The remainder of the book's plot skillfully alternates among multiple parallel plot lines, the most involving and interesting of which depicts Amariah's integration into the rebel group. Prior to being thrust into their midst, Amariah has known of the rebels only from frightened accounts given by those who have faced them in battle. For their part, most of the rebels have loathed Amariah for his wealth and his involvement in making biofuels, so much so that their leader initially sees fit to have a guard accompany him at all times for his own protection. (While the rebels generally acknowledge that Amariah was at least committed to *responsibly producing biofuels*, this makes him deserving only of lesser-of-two-evils status in their eyes, since they're against biofuels period.) However, as Amariah and his newfound companions get to know one another, a mutual fondness develops, and eventually Amariah finds himself becoming a key strategist behind an insurrection they mount against the Yorkers.

Fehling says a big part of what attracts him to science fiction is its potential to spark dialog about important issues facing humanity. And indeed, with *Dark Peak* he aims to get readers talking about one of the most vital, but also least understood, dimensions of our society's energy situation: the issue of steadily declining net energy. With each passing year, we're further exhausting Earth's stores of the highly concentrated forms of fossil energy necessary for industrial economies, as well as further deluding ourselves into believing that the dregs left behind will be anywhere near adequate to power civilization as we know it. Fehling seeks to show why these "alternative" energy sources won't be up to the task, and why even attempting the exercise could result in entire forests being denuded within a single human lifetime.

Dark Peak is Fehling's first novel, and it's a promising debut. The author succeeds in his stated goals of telling an engaging tale and warning of the ecological threat that he sees coming. The premise is original and intriguing; the plot, fast-paced and suspenseful. There's a satisfying character arc for our protagonist and even a swell coming-of-age romance.

My sole criticism is that the villains and the fictional world could have been more solidly developed. Still, it's a measure of Fehling's skill overall that I welcome the chance to see if he can improve on this in any follow-up books that he may publish down the line.

Interested in submitting stories to MYTHIC? We prefer electronic submissions. You may email us at the following address:

submissions@mythicmag.com

We do accept paper submissions. You can send them to the following address:

Shaun Kilgore
MYTHIC Submissions
420 Commercial Street
Danville, IL 61832

For more complete submission guidelines and any other information you may visit our website:

www.mythicmag.com

69389761R00074

Made in the USA
Columbia, SC
12 April 2017